'T   SE

'T   ely told'

Class. of   THE SUNDAY TRIBUNE

A novel set in contemporary Ireland, by the author of
the CHILDREN OF THE FAMINE TRILOGY
Under the Hawthorn Tree, *Wildflower Girl* and *Fields of Home*.

Having lived in a caravan as a traveller, Katie settles in a new
house with her family and begins a new life. She must deal with
great changes and with big challenges. She has high hopes, but
many obstacles are put in her way. It is difficult for her to find new
friends and to fit into a new school. Luckily, Katie has
courage and guts – she will not give up easily.

**Marita Conlon-McKenna's books have remained
on the bestseller lists for many years. They have also sold in
the USA, Britain, Australia and Canada,
and have been translated into many languages.**

Special Merit Award to The O'Brien Press
from **Reading Association of Ireland**
*'for exceptional care, skill and professionalism in
publishing, resulting in a consistently high standard in all
of the children's books published by The O'Brien Press'*

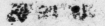

MARITA CONLON-McKENNA is one of
Ireland's most popular children's authors. She
has written eight best-selling books to date, and
they have been translated into many languages.
Under the Hawthorn Tree, her first novel, became an immediate bestseller and has been de-
scribed as 'the biggest success story in children's
historical fiction'. Its sequels, *Wildflower Girl* and
Fields of Home, which complete the *Children of
the Famine* trilogy, have also been hugely suc-
cessful. Marita lives in Dublin with her husband
and four children.

Other books by

Marita Conlon-McKenna

Granny MacGinty

Under the Hawthorn Tree

Wildflower Girl

Fields of Home

No Goodbye

Safe Harbour

In Deep Dark Wood

Under the Hawthorn Tree is also available on video

the Blue Horse

Marita Conlon-McKenna

THE O'BRIEN PRESS
DUBLIN

First published 1992 by The O'Brien Press Ltd,
20 Victoria Road, Dublin 6, Ireland.
Tel: +353 1 4923333; Fax: +353 1 4922777
E-mail: books@obrien.ie
Website: www.obrien.ie
Reprinted 1993 (twice), 1996, 1998, 2001, 2003.

ISBN 0-86278-305-4

British Library Cataloguing-in-Publication Data
Conlon-McKenna, Marita
Blue Horse
I. Title
823.914 [J]

7 8 9 10 11
03 04 05 06 07

The O'Brien Press receives
assistance from

Typesetting, layout, editing, design: The O'Brien Press Ltd
Cover frontispiece drawing: Donald Teskey
Printing: Cox & Wyman Ltd

CONTENTS

'Hold your head high.'

With gratitude to the Arts Council
for the Creative Literature Bursary which enabled
me to research and write this book.
Thanks to all those who took the time and
trouble to talk to me.

Chapter 1
SUMMERTIME

Katie looked out of the car window as it swerved off the main road and bumped up over the grass verge. It began to push through the gap in the hedgerow. She pressed her face against the glass as the branches and leaves and wild briars scraped against the windows.

The stoney ground sloped down to a field where other caravans and trailers lay spread about.

'Here we are!' announced her father, with a huge sigh of relief as the car came to a standstill. Three dogs ran forward, yapping and jumping with curiosity.

In the back of the car they all began to yawn and stretch. Part of Katie's leg had gone dead and she tried to work her foot backwards and forwards to get the circulation going.

'Come on, you lot, out you get!' Da got out and pulled the car doors wide open.

One by one they clambered out. A crowd of children ran over and a big black labrador pushed his cold nose against Katie, slobbering all over her clean jeans. She smiled. Mister belonged to her Uncle Mike.

'Down, Mister! Down, good dog! I know you're glad to see me.'

Straight away the twins shot off and were soon running around the place exploring. Her mother got out of the front seat slowly with little Davey asleep in her arms.

The door of one of the trailers was flung open and a woman jumped down onto the grass. Auntie Brigid. She ran over to greet them. Katie waved towards some of her cousins grinning in the middle of a group of muddy children of all sizes. The twins were going to love it here.

'Katie, stir yourself and give me a hand,' urged her mother.'Take hold of Hannah. She's nervous of all the strangers and fuss.'

Impatiently Katie grabbed at the sticky fingers of her shy, seven-year-old sister. 'Come on, you big baby, nobody's going to bite you!'

Hannah stared at her. Her pale golden hair blew in the breeze and framed a round, innocent face. Katie relented. How could anyone be cross with such an angel, she thought guiltily.

While Mam and Auntie Brigid stood chatting, Da got back into the car and set about trying to find a suitable spot for their caravan. Soon he and Katie's fourteen-year-old brother, Tom, had reversed into a shady corner and they began to unhook the trailer. Da heaved out the large yellow bottle of gas and connected it up.

A tall well-built girl, with wavy blond hair, called them over to their aunt's large trailer, with all its frills and flounces and brightly polished windows. Everything seemed to be in its place as usual in the neat caravan.

'Hi, Maggie!'

'Hiya, Katie. Will you have a drop of lemonade? We've some biscuits as well.' She passed them around. The twins, as if by magic, appeared and gulped down their drinks, standing on the step, and then ran off again with the gang.

'Paddy, Brian, listen to me! Take care running around – you don't know this place yet, so have a bit of care!' shouted Mam as the two red-heads disappeared down the field.

'They'll be grand, Kathleen, don't be bothering yourself about them,' said Auntie Brigid reassuringly. 'My lot'll keep an eye out for them. You just enjoy the tea and tell me all the news since we last met.'

Maggie glanced at Katie and cast her eyes upwards. Obviously a long gossip-session. 'Are you coming outside, Katie?'

Hannah followed them and the three girls sat on the step outside the door. The sun was weakening and there was a slight nip in the air.

'This is a fine place,' Katie said, glancing around the field.

'You should have seen it in the middle of winter. We were up to our knees in mud, but in the good weather it's great,' agreed Maggie.

'I think it's lovely,' Hannah declared solemnly. 'I hope we stay here for a long, long time.'

'Well, there's no telling how long any of us will stay any place,' said her cousin, 'but let's make the most of it! Do you see the big trees over there? About ten minutes on there's a little stream. You might catch a few pinkeens in it. Do you have a net?'

Hannah shook her head.

'Well, we're handy to the town. We'll get you one there.'

Katie looked all around her. Clothes-lines had been strung between two or three of the tall trees and clothes flapped, drying in the breeze. Two multicoloured blankets were spread out to air on the grass. At one end of the field were three broken-down scrap cars, one without wheels. A cock and a few hens ran around the place, scratching and squawking. Almost at the centre of the camp was the telltale circle of stones and sticks and ashes and coals. A fire. Tonight, maybe, there'd be a fire lit. Katie hoped so.

Tom came striding over, carrying their puppy in his arms. 'Katie, will you hold Duffy? She has us tormented trying to set up.'

'Duffy, be a good dog. What have you been up to?' asked Katie as the dog began to gnaw at her hands.

'Teething is she?' laughed Maggie. 'She's a grand little thing – a terrier is it?'

'Sort of,' said Katie, tossing Duffy onto the grass. Straight away the dog began to pull at Hannah's shoelaces. Hannah jumped up and raced backwards and forwards, the dog trailing after her.

Tom was busy taking stuff from the boot of the car. At fourteen he was a smaller and thinner version of his father. His hair had darkened from fair to brown and his grey-green eyes seemed to be always searching for something when you were talking to him. He loved to be with Da, and the two of them were great friends.

After about an hour, Mam came out onto the top step of her sister's caravan. 'I'd better go and get things sorted out, I suppose,' she announced. 'Thanks a lot, Brigid, 'tis real nice to be back together again. Here, Katie, take Davey and mind him. Hannah, you come with me. You can help set the table and sweep out the place.'

Katie smiled to herself. Mam seemed happy to be near Brigid's family again. A summer here would do them all good. This was what travelling was all about. Fresh air and being your own boss, and finding a bit of space for yourself with plenty of friends around. And if you were lucky nobody to evict you or tell you to move on.

'Katie! Katie! Are you gone deaf? Honest, you're a right dreamer. Do you want to come for a walk after tea and see the place?'

'Oh sorry, Maggie, I was miles away. Yeah, that would be great. I'll see you later, then. Come on, Davey.'

Carrying her baby brother, Katie made her way towards the brown and cream caravan. Mam stood watching as Da hammered a thick pole into the ground to one side of the door. Mam unwrapped the small blanket she was holding, then carefully took out a carved wooden horse and fixed it securely on top of the pole.

The blue painted horse stood looking out over the camp. No matter where they travelled or camped, once everything was set up, Mam would always take out her most prized possession and put it up as a sign that this was their place now, if only for a few days. The trees, the earth, the water, the air around them would be a part of them for the time they needed it until they moved on again.

Davey looked at the blue horse.

'Hossey, hossey,' he babbled.

'That means home, Davey. The blue horse means home,' Katie told him proudly.

Chapter 2
A STRANGER

Hannah helped Katie to wash up after tea and stack the plates and cups away, while Mam changed Davey into his soft blue pyjamas. The twins stood on the seats and got the pillows and blankets and sheets out of the overhead sliding cupboards.

'No bouncing or pillow fights!' warned Mam. 'Tom, will you go over and ask Brigid for a drop of water so we'll have enough for later. In the morning we'll have to get the containers filled.'

The sun slowly dipped behind a cluster of trees, tingeing the evening sky with a warm rosy glow. Katie noticed two men bent down lighting the fire.

Mam, satisfied that all the beds were ready, pulled on her warm 'night' cardigan and stepped outside. A chance to chat and relax under the stars always put her in a good humour. She helped the other women spread a few rugs on the grass.

It surprised Katie when Maggie appeared, looking very grown-up and pretty. She had changed her clothes, tied up her blond hair, and two golden leaf-shapes dangled from her ears.

'Come on, Katie! Let's get out of here and go for a walk.'

'I'm coming too,' Hannah announced.

'No! You're not!' groaned Katie in exasperation. 'Leave us alone.'

She was fed up with her sister always hanging around. She wanted to be with her own friends, free of the younger ones for a while.

'Bridey, come over here,' shouted Maggie. A girl of about eight, her jet black plaits flying out behind her, broke away from the gang.

'Bridey, this is our cousin Hannah. Do you remember her?' Bridey grinned, showing a mouthful of missing teeth. 'Now, I'm putting you in charge of minding her and making sure the others play with her!'

Bridey nodded and pulled the reluctant Hannah towards a group of girls pushing a broken-down pram in the fading light.

'She'll be fine. Come on.'

Maggie led the way down a dirt path, past the other caravans and trailers, avoiding two rubbish piles. They crossed a long, narrow field where a few ponies and horses grazed. The mares stared drowsily at the girls and the gangly foals whinnied, looking for attention.

Light was fading fast as they wandered into a small wood, keeping their mouths shut as they passed through a curtain of thousands of tiny midges.

Finally, they reached a spot where ancient oak trees almost formed a circle – the perfect hideaway. From the huge, sturdy branches of the largest oak, three old black tyres dangled and a few heavy ropes hung enticingly. The best swing in the whole country.

Katie couldn't resist it and clambered up on the base of the tree and onto a tyre – forcing it backwards and forwards with her body weight.

'It's great.' She laughed as she whistled through the air and the thick greenness of the leaves. 'Come on, Maggie.'

Maggie just stood on the grass and looked up at her. 'Yeah, the kids love it.' Her voice was wistful.

Maggie would once have been first to climb to the very tip-top of the tree, but something had changed her. Katie let the silence fall between them, unsure what to say.

'Did I tell you I got a job?'

Katie looked surprised.

'I'm learning to sew on a big machine. It's good money, too, and a good training.'

'What do you sew?'

'Jeans, shirts, curtains. Someone else cuts them out and we put them together. God, I bet you never thought you'd see the day.'

Katie smiled nervously.

'It's up in the town. One of the Caseys works there too. Fellas and girls, so it's good fun ... ' she stopped.

'Maggie, come up and have a go,' Katie pleaded, pushing a tyre in her direction.

'That's just kids' stuff!' Maggie shrugged. 'Anyway, we'd better get back. It's getting dark.'

Katie, making a great effort, swung higher and higher, aiming at the tip of a twisted branch that hung out beyond all the others.

'Suit yourself! I'm off,' Maggie shouted.

With a lurch, Katie managed to tap the branch at last with the tip of her shoe, then slowed down the movement of the swing till she could jump off and run after her cousin. She didn't want to be left alone in the dark strangeness of this wood.

*　　*　　*

Hours later, in the stillness of the night, something stirred. It roused Katie. The whole camp was quiet. The fire had died down and everyone was asleep. A shadow seemed to flit by the caravan window. Maybe it was a cloud racing across the moon, or a bat.

Katie sat up and peered out. Everything looked blurred. Black silhouettes of bushes and hedges seemed threatening in the dark. She heard a rustling sound. There was definitely something outside. Duffy gave a low growl. The dog was supposed to sleep outside the caravan, but usually ended up snuggled in with the twins in their bed. Mam turned a blind eye.

A footfall. She thought she heard the grass crunch under a shoe.

Who was outside?

Katie was scared. Should she call Mam and Da? Or was she just imagining things? She pulled back from the window, hoping she could not be seen. No one else stirred. She strained her eyes. There was movement outside ... definitely ... it was ... a man ... no ... a boy. In the moonlight his face looked white, almost like a ghost. His eyes were two dark smudges. His thick hair stood on end. A loose-fitting shirt hung out over cropped jeans.

He was moving nearer. She barely dared to breathe. Oh no! He was standing in front of the blue horse. He stared at it intently. Was he going to steal it? Katie sat mesmerised, watching the boy.

He stretched out his hand towards the wooden horse. He traced the line of its head and back, its legs and long flowing tail. He felt the horse from top to bottom, making no effort to lift it off. He turned around, his eyes searching for something.

It was too late – he'd spotted her through the window in the moonlight. She felt like an animal caught in the glare of a headlight as they stared at each other. This strange boy – he disturbed her. For an instant they studied each other. Then he seemed to drop down towards the ground where something was scrabbling around outside. She hoped it wasn't rats.

A second or two later he stood up again. He held a young kid goat in his arms and he seemed to be talking to it, soothing it. He began to walk away, and then, without warning, he turned back and waved at her. She wasn't sure if he was saying hello or goodbye as he disappeared in the dark.

Chapter 3
THE GOAT BOY

She had almost forgotten about the boy next morning, when a knock came on the door. Katie opened it a fraction. With a start, she saw it was him. She flushed, and stood, confused, not saying anything.

'Hiya, Francis,' shouted Paddy from behind her.

'My grandmother sent me over to show you where to go for water,' he said. 'The water in the stream isn't clean enough for drinking.'

'We'll be ready in a minute. Come on, Brian! Come on, Katie! Where are my shoes?'

Francis waited outside in the sunshine for them. Katie pulled on a T-shirt and shorts and a pair of runners – she found a wide navy hairband she shared with Hannah and hoped it would help keep some of her mass of red hair out of her eyes.

The sunlight almost blinded her as she stepped outside.

Francis stood in front of the blue horse, running his fingers along the smooth, painted wood.

'It's beautiful.'

'Yeah,' agreed Katie.

'What's it for?' he asked.

'The horse is my Mam's. Her granddaddy made it for her when she was a little girl.'

'Oh, a kind of souvenir then.'

'No, it's much more than that.' She tried to explain. 'My great-grandfather, like his father before him, used to make the old-fashioned wagons. They travelled all the roads of Ireland and made homes for lots of the travelling families, and on a small corner of every wagon they always painted a blue horse so that people would know who the maker was. My great-grandfather carved this wooden one for Mam. The old wagons are gone but we still have our blue horse and no matter where we camp Mam puts him up for luck and in memory of times past. She says we must never forget those times, and that the blue horse brings us good fortune.'

Francis nodded. 'Gran is the same. She gets strange feelings about places and people, about what is good luck and bad luck, and where we should camp or not.'

'Some people say she has second sight,' he added. 'She can tell fortunes, and all around her she sees signs that the rest of us don't notice.'

'Hurry up, Katie,' shouted Paddy, swinging a water container towards her. Katie grabbed it, then she and Francis fell into step. She forced herself to keep up with his long strides. He was much taller than her and she guessed he was a year or two older.

They came to a large white house with a neat driveway bordered with multicoloured flowers. Francis told everyone to stop, then he ran up and rang the doorbell.

No one answered.

'Ah hell, the lady must be out. We'll have to come back again.'

'What about the other houses? Can't we try them?'

He looked uncertain.

'I'll try,' suggested Katie.

Two or three modern redbrick houses stood beside each other. Katie went up and knocked at the first door. Through the window she could see the children watching a large television set. It was blaring loudly. She knocked again. One of the girls got up, came out and answered the door.

'Yeah, what is it?' she demanded.

'Could you help us, please?' Katie lifted up the large white plastic container. 'We need some drinking water as –'

The girl half-closed the door and shouted up the stairs.

'Mum, it's a gypsy, she wants something.'

Katie couldn't hear the reply.

The girl reopened the door wider.

'Sorry, we've nothing for you.'

'It's only water –' Katie began.

The girl was not listening and shut the door quickly.

Katie noticed her go back to the television set. At the next house a man was busy mowing the small front lawn. As they got nearer he switched off the mower, strode towards the garden gate and banged it shut. Then, turning his back towards them, he started up the machine, its loud noise breaking the quiet of the morning.

The twins knocked on the door of the last house.

A smartly-dressed woman answered the door.

'I'm sorry, I'm rushing out.'

'Please, Miss,' Francis pleaded, 'we only need some water. We're camped down the road a bit.'

'Look, I'm sorry, but I'm in a bit of a hurry. Why don't you try next door?'

She came out onto the front step, pulled the door shut after her, and with her keys and bag in her hand quickly got into the small silver car in the driveway and drove out the gateway in the direction of the town. They stood watching her, still clutching the empty plastic containers in their hands.

'Best get back,' murmured Francis.

'Mam'll kill us if we've no water,' said Brian.

'Look, we'll try later,' said Katie, irritated.

As they walked back towards the camp they noticed a car in the driveway of the first house.

'Will we try again?' asked Katie.

'No harm,' laughed Francis, going up and ringing the bell.

A middle-aged woman opened the door. Her eyes brightened when she saw Francis.

'It's the boy from down the road, isn't it? More water I suppose!'

He nodded. 'We called earlier. These are the Connors. They moved in yesterday and need some water too, if that's all right.'

A shadow seemed to pass over her face – maybe she thought she'd be swamped with travellers looking for water now – but was quickly blown away. She brought them into a small room off the kitchen, where there was a washing machine, a tumble-drier and an ironing board, and one shelf was stacked with washing powder and cleaning stuff.

Francis had already started to fill his container, placing it in the large sink and running the tap. The others copied him when he had finished. The lady of the house disappeared back into the kitchen.

When they had filled up, Francis knocked on the kitchen door.

'Well, I hope that's all right for you all,' the woman said.

They smiled and thanked her. She handed them a packet of biscuits.

'Have one each.' They were chocolate chip.

'Look, Francis, if I'm out when you call and you need water, why don't you leave the containers on the step outside this door and when I get home I'll fill them for you and you can collect them later.'

'That's very nice of you, Ma'am.' Francis blushed.

'With this heat, everyone needs plenty of water. It's the least I can do.' She smiled kindly.

Thanking her again, they left and began to walk back to the camp.

The full containers were really heavy. The twins carried one between them, stopping every few seconds to have a rest. Katie hadn't quite filled hers, as she knew if it was more than three-quarters full it was impossible to lift.

It seemed ages before they got back to the campsite. The glaring sun highlighted the peeling paint and the ramshackle condition of many of the caravans. Some were new and shiny and stood out like sore thumbs.

With the heat of the day the rubbish around the site had begun to smell and clouds of buzzing flies hung heavy in the air. Katie hoped there weren't any rats.

Francis helped her lift the water up into the kitchen.

'Would you like to see the goats and meet my Gran?' he asked.

She looked at Mam.

'That's all right, Katie, once you're back in the middle of the day,' Mam said.

Katie followed Francis as he wound his way through the field and down towards a small sea-green caravan, that reminded her of an egg-box. An elderly woman lay stretched out on a battered-looking deckchair making the most of the fine day, whilst keeping up a conversation with a pure white goat that grazed beside her.

'Delighted to meet you.'

For an instant Katie wasn't sure if the woman was talking to the goat or to Katie herself. But Nan Maguire's welcoming handshake reassured her.

'The Connors girl, is it?' she said, searching the young girl's face.

Katie took an immediate liking to this old traveller woman. Her grey hair was pulled back in a bun and she wore a striped T-shirt and a floral skirt. Her face was lined but looked happy. But it was her eyes that attracted Katie like a magnet – they were the colour of the sky overhead, and when they focused on Katie, she felt as if the old woman could see right into her, to her very soul.

'Kathleen – yes it's a good traveller name. My grandson Francis here is named after the good saint who loved all the animals. Naming is important.'

Katie looked at the ground, unsure what to say.

'Come on. I'll show you the rest of the herd,' Francis offered, leading the way to where a makeshift pen held some of the goats.

Two were not much more than kids and they stared at her with huge clear eyes and pushed against her clothes looking for a loose end to grab and nibble or chew.

'That's Gertie, and this is Old George. Be careful of him, he's a bit cross. And these two are Goosey and Gilly. The rest of them are up on the hillside.'

Katie touched them gingerly at first.

'Some people give goats a bad name but I like them,' Francis declared. 'Ever since I came back here to live with my Gran when I was nine, I've helped with them. So I've been at it this past six years.'

Katie smiled to herself – they were almost the same age then.

When he talked about the goats his face kind of lit up. 'People from the town often come to the field inquiring about the goats' milk. It's meant to be great for children and babies who are allergic to cows' milk. If we had a piece of land and a whole load of goats I'd say there'd be plenty of money in it.' Suddenly he stopped as if he had said too much, given his hopes away. 'Let's get back – it must be one o'clock.'

*   *   *

Day after day Katie seemed to spend more and more time with the 'goat-boy', as Mam had nick-named him. He was a good listener and she told him about all the towns they had visited, and about Sister Mary in the national school who had helped her to learn to read and write.

It was a strange thing being a traveller that even though you were always surrounded by your own family and the other families on a site, it was very hard to become a really good friend with anyone, to have someone special to talk to. The minute you got friendly with someone they could suddenly go off to the far side of Ireland. Sometimes Katie felt very lonely. In the last two schools she had gone to, she had noticed the way the other girls all had a best friend. She had found herself always on the outside of that. Now at night and even when she was washing the cups she wondered if a boy could be a girl's best friend. Were Mam and Da best friends once?

Francis told her all about himself and his grand-mother. He was very fond of animals, knew more than a hundred books would tell you. He and his gran were always moving.

Nan Maguire's fame as a fortune teller was known far and wide. Every Tuesday, when the other women went off begging door-to-door, all sorts of people would make their way to the tiny caravan and spend between fifteen and thirty minutes having their fortune told. On sunny days, the crowds of giggling girls and older, worried-looking women waiting their turn would sit on a fallen tree trunk that served as a bench. If it was cold they sat in groups or in cars up on the road.

Some of the others living on the site resented the old woman's way of making a living and were jealous when they saw the crowds every week.

'More power to her, that's what I say,' Mam declared firmly.

'Do you think she has the gift really, Mam? Do you believe it?' asked Katie.

'Indeed I do. There are lots of our people touched with gifts – nature meant it so.' She looked at Katie. 'Those people that come to her may have lost their way a bit. Someone to help them put a foot on the right path or tell them the strings to break – that can only be a good thing.'

'Has she told your fortune, Mam?'

'No, lovey, I know my fortune. I got the man I love and I got the children I love. I'd be afraid what I might hear, so it's best left well alone.'

As every day passed Katie longed more and more to get Nan to tell what lay in store for her.

Chapter 4
THE FORTUNE TELLING

An icecream! Katie longed for something cool.

> *I scream!*
> *You scream!*
> *We all scream*
> *For icecream!*

The chant went up among the younger children and Katie ended up taking Hannah and two of the cousins on a walk about a mile up the road to the shops. It was sweltering. Davey sat in the old buggy and the rest of them walked slowly in the heat.

The small newsagent and sweetshop was set in the middle of a cluster of houses. Prices were far too high for the weekly groceries but they went there for the odd thing. When they got through the heavy swing door they all stood at the icecream cabinet looking at the pictures and trying to decide which one to choose.

Two boys aged about eleven or twelve came in after them and stood near the biscuit shelf watching them.

'I want an orange ice-pop,' Katie's cousin Miley decided.

'Hannah and I want a choc-ice,' said Bridey.

'Chocky,' gabbled Davey, waving his fat little hands in the air.

Katie slid back the top of the cabinet and put her hand down to get the icecreams.

'Jeepers, look at that dirty tinker putting her filthy hands into the icecream,' said one of the boys, pointing at her.

'That's gross,' his fat friend added.

A waft of cold air from the fridge chilled Katie while at the same time a tingle of fear stabbed at her.

'Look at these cute little plaits!' The first boy came up behind Bridey and tugged at her hair.

'Let me go, you're hurting me,' pleaded Bridey, her head at an angle trying to avoid the pain.

'Leave those children alone.' The shopkeeper came out from behind the counter. Bridey broke free and ran up near the buggy.

Katie pulled the money out of the pocket of her shorts to pay for all the icecreams and quick as lightning pushed Davey and the rest of them back outside onto the footpath. They walked along cautiously and had only just started to eat their icecreams when they spotted the two boys on their bikes, cycling up towards them.

Katie stopped and pretended to tie her shoelace, hoping the bikes would pass by, but instead they slowed and stopped right in front of them.

'A hole in your shoe, is that it?' one of them taunted. Katie blushed, but tried to avoid their eyes and push Davey on.

'Have you got that pen-knife, Conor? I fancy that little black plait – you can have the other!' Horrified, Katie swung around. One of the boys had grabbed Bridey and was making scissor actions with his fingers at her hair. Furious, Bridey was trying to kick out at him.

'Dirty tramps,' jeered one of the fellas. 'Knackers!'

'We're not tramps,' said Katie, 'we're travellers.'

The boys didn't listen.

'Let go of her,' Katie demanded.

'Buzz off, Ginger,' one of the boys shouted at her.

'I'll hit him for you, Katie,' Miley said. Even at ten he looked only half the size of the other fellow.

'No, Miley, just keep quiet. We don't want any trouble.'

Suddenly – how it happened Katie didn't know – Hannah ran forward and kicked the boy holding Bridey in the stomach. 'Take that, you big bully,' she screamed.

Shocked and winded, he let go.

Quick as a flash, Katie rammed the two boys with Davey in the buggy, his melting chocolate icecream staining their T-shirts.

'Run for it,' she shouted to the others and made a second ramming attack, this time at the bicycles which she shoved off the path. They clattered and scraped as they fell into the road.

Then she took to her heels with Davey frantically trying to hold on to what was left of his icecream.

She was half-waiting for the boys to grab her, but then she realised a car was hooting – the driver had almost run over the bikes and was out of his car shouting at the boys.

'Run! Run! Run! Keep running!' she yelled at them all.

They were exhausted by the time they got to the campsite. Hannah was limping slightly as she had fallen in the rush and badly grazed her knee and hands. She had surprised them all with her burst of bravery. But by the time they reached home, huge, heaving, gulping breaths were taking her over and she was shaking. She was so white Katie could see the veins under her eyes.

God, wouldn't you know it. Mam wasn't there. Hannah was crying now for all the world to hear. Miley and Bridey were telling everyone about the bully boys.

'Bring her over to me, Katie!'

Nan Maguire was standing at the door of her little caravan with a mug of tea in her hand. Katie handed Hannah up to her. Luckily Davey had fallen asleep with all the excitement, and she moved the buggy so that part of him lay in the shade. She hoped a bee wouldn't come along and sting him, he was so sticky.

'Uh, uh, uh,' sobbed Hannah.

'Hush, hush. Little Hannah, isn't it?'

Hannah nodded.

'Sit down here quiet a minute.'

She led Hannah inside to the small seat under the window. It was covered with multicoloured cushions. The old lady took Hannah by the hand and began to stroke her hand, then her arm and finally stood near her rubbing her shoulder.

'Let the tension go, pet, cry it out, no need to be scared, pet, you're safe here with Katie and me.'

Hannah sniffed and tried to catch her breath.

The stroking kept on going round and round in circles and almost in time to it Hannah's breathing slowed and steadied.

'Put on the kettle there for more tea, Katie, and wet that old towel a bit till I cool off Hannah's face.'

Taking the damp material she dabbed gently at Hannah's tear-stained, dirty face.

'Now, a nice cup of milky tea, always good after a shock.'

Through the window, Katie could spot Bridey jumping around, trying to see what was going on. Noticing her, Hannah began to brighten up.

'I hear you're a great brave girl,' murmured Nan. 'Is that true?'

Suddenly shy, Hannah whispered, 'I suppose.'

'No supposin' about it. Let me look at your hand, lovey.' She turned the small hand over each way. The fingers long and narrow, the nails cut unevenly and in need of a good scrub.

'Hmmm.'

Katie moved closer. Hannah's eyes were wide and her lips were open with wonder.

'Destined to give love and be loved, a good strong heart that will fight for those you love. Some clouds, some mists, but yet I see the sunshine always shining through for you. I see music and song and a time to dance and play. Good fortune, sweet girl.' She stopped. Hannah was enraptured.

'Is there any more?' she pleaded.

'You're too young yet to speak of that far ahead, but you will marry. This is not the hand of an old maid.'

Once her hand was let go, Hannah jumped up. 'I must tell Bridey.'

The old lady tried to look serious and hide her smile. 'Away off with you now. I'm glad you're feeling better.'

Pushing the door out, the little girl disappeared. Katie wordlessly took her place. Nan stared at her. It's my turn now, thought Katie.

'Will you tell my fortune please, Mrs Maguire?'

Taking a sip of tea from her mug, the old lady looked straight into Katie's eyes. Katie spread her hand on one of the cushions. Nan lifted it and studied it.

Katie's hands were rounded, the fingers fairly long but broad at the tips; her nails were slightly bitten and she realised that the back of her hand still had a bit of dried icecream on it.

'Working hands, hard-working hands, toil but yet at times able to be gentle, caring. A long lifeline and a good life, hard but good. Changes, a lot of changes.'

'What kind of changes?' Katie asked nervously. It was obvious, being a traveller and moving from place to place, that there would be changes.

Nan was staring at her hand and then locked her eyes to Katie's.

'Changes of the heart, changes of the soul even.

Things destroyed.' Nan stopped. A frown ran across her forehead. 'Something loved destroyed, an animal I think, I'm not sure.' Nan's voice was slow and the girl knew she was being cautious with the words. Fortune tellers never gave bad news.

'My future,' Katie pleaded. 'Is it bad?'

The older woman seemed to become more businesslike. 'There will be marriage and family, all you have ever wanted, nothing will come that easy, but you will find and marry the man you love.'

Katie let out a sigh of relief.

Davey had begun to wail outside. She stood up to go to him, but the woman still held her hand. 'Katie, follow your instincts, trust to them and they will see you right.'

She nodded. Her instincts. She didn't rightly understand what Nan meant and right now she wasn't even sure she was going to have good fortune.

'Remember, Katie, follow your own instincts always.' Nan stood and started to tidy up her caravan.

A shaft of sunlight flooded in the door. Davey lay half-awake, one arm flung across his face to protect it from the bright sun. This arm was already burned red.

'Thanks, Mrs Maguire, thanks for everything.'

Katie had a feeling that the old woman hadn't told her half of what she had seen in her hand.

Chapter 5
STICKS AND STONES

'It's not fair. Those boys started it.'

'If I can't trust you to bring the kids to the shop and get them home safely, there'll be no more shops,' Mam pronounced firmly.

'But I didn't do anything,' pleaded Katie.

'The bully boys did it, Mam, they called us knackers and tinkers and followed us,' Hannah added.

'I'm not talking to you, Hannah, this is between me and Katie.'

'But Katie did nothing,' her little sister kept on.

'Listen, I don't care what those boys said, you should know well now: Sticks and stones ... '

Katie lifted her eyes to heaven: Sticks and stones may break my bones, but words will never hurt me. It was one of their mother's, and for that matter their father's, favourite sayings. No matter what people called you or shouted at you or how they insulted you, just ignore it.

'I didn't cause trouble, Mam, I swear I didn't,' Katie promised. 'They followed us. One of the boys was going to cut off Bridey's hair, he was hurting her ...'

'No trouble. Is that too much to ask of a big girl like yourself, not to cause or bring us trouble?' Mam kept on. 'No trouble is it, letting your little sister kick a big boy?'

'I did it myself, I just couldn't stand it another

second,' shouted Hannah.

'But the worst of it, to use an innocent baby, a little child, my own little man, as a battle weapon! Your father will kill you if he hears of it.'

'But he didn't get hurt, Mam, he wasn't crying or anything,' answered Katie.

'Your little sister all bruised and cut and upset and the baby terrified out of his wits, what kind of a girl are you?'

Katie was silent.

A barrage of words built up in her brain. She knew if she said one word they would all be forced out like a flood. Why should they keep out of trouble, never reply, walk away? She stayed silent.

'And then the worst of it – getting your fortune told while the baby was being roasted alive in the sun. Nearly a quarter of a bottle of calamine lotion I've had to rub on him.'

'I'm sorry, Mam.'

'Hmm!'

'It wasn't Mrs Maguire's fault. She helped us because you weren't here. Hannah needed calming down ...'

'She was real nice to me too, Mam,' added Hannah.

'Now I suppose I'll have to go down and thank her for her help. I will say this and listen to me the both of you, and you, boys, too –' the twins and Tom were watching a black-and-white portable television up at the front end of the trailer, '– keep out of trouble. There will be enough bad things that will find their way to your door, so walk away from trouble, take another road, go the long way, don't reply, don't answer back. Are ye all listening?'

Katie nodded.

'Yes, Mam,' Hannah smiled nervously.

The boys grunted some kind of answer, despite being engrossed in the TV programme. Mam seemed satisfied.

'Now let that be an end to it and none of you are to let me down.' She got the brush and began to brush Hannah's hair.

*   *   *

At the end of the week Francis and his grandmother got ready to leave. Katie couldn't believe it. Her new friend! He came to say goodbye.

'Do you really have to go?' she asked.

He nodded. He was rubbing two or three leaves between his fingers.

'Is it because of the goats?' she said, thinking it was funny how a person could suddenly go off goats, take a strong dislike to them in fact.

He shrugged. 'They need fresh grass, some wild herbs.' He paused. 'Look, Katie, you know what Gran's like. She gets notions about things – about places – she's just a superstitious old woman. The goats are part of it but she has a real feeling we must leave this place.'

Francis stood so close to her, his arm stretched out above her as he pulled more leaves from the ivy trailing over the wall behind them. Her head came just about to his chin. A dart of loneliness pricked her.

'We're going to Galway – it's nice there. Gran always likes it. In about two weeks there'll be a summer fair, plenty of people, horses, games and stalls, buying and selling!

'Maybe you'll all get up to Galway.' He tried to sound cheerful.

'Maybe.' She fixed her eyes on one of the dogs stretched out on the grass in the distance. She could see the alsatian's stomach going up and down, his tongue out; she could almost hear his panting.

'Are you listening to me, Katie?'

His hand now rested on her shoulder.

'Our paths will cross again, you can depend on it.' She looked into his eyes and knew he was not just saying it, they were not empty words.

'I hope so,' she whispered.

'I promise,' he said, before turning and running off back down the field.

At midday a car and a small lorry appeared, and the goats were loaded in. Francis was sitting in the front seat with the driver. Nan got into the car which would tow the small caravan. In a small procession they left Kilcross. To Katie the place seemed strangely empty.

Chapter 6
JUMP!

'I'm going to have a game of cards with Brigid,'
announced Mam.

Katie nodded. She was glad to see Mam going
out, even if it was just next door for an hour or so.
The men kept disappearing off every night and it
was lonely for her.

'Be good,' Mam called.

Katie was busy sorting out a pile of socks that
didn't match. Tom lay on his bunk with a magazine
of pictures of motorbikes. He loved looking at
them and having them all around him while he
slept. With bits of sellotape he stuck up pictures of
fellas and girls on all kinds of big bikes. He could
name all the bikes, even though he wasn't too hot
at reading and most of the names were foreign-
sounding and meant nothing to the others.

She could hear him tearing a page or two out.

'Katie, pass me in the sellotape, will you?'

'Get it yourself, I'm busy,' she retorted.

'Ah go on, have a look for it.'

She pulled out one or two drawers under the
food cupboard. 'It's not here,' she called.

'It must be,' he shouted.

'I see it – it's all gone.' She flung the small, empty
cardboard circle at him. 'The twins must have been
at it.'

She could hear him moving around and the

creak of his bunk as he swung himself down.

'I'm going over to Pat's trailer. I won't be long.'

The caravan was quiet, the others chatting in low tones, their eyes locked on the black-and-white images from the TV.

Suddenly the light seemed to flicker. Katie went to stand up. Maybe the bottle of gas was nearly empty, but with a burst of brightness it settled back again. She ignored it.

Then a strange crackling sound came from the kitchen. She slid the door open more. Where was the noise coming from? The kitchen seemed bright, too bright. The mantle had fallen from the gas light, and an inch of fire ran from one flimsy curtain to the other. The lower half of the window was blackened, and the wood surround was being licked by a tongue of vivid orange flames. She grabbed the kettle of water off the cooker and flung it at the window. Black smoke hissed at her, but like a creature scuttling away from an attacker, a burst of fire ran in a line along the panelling and took flight across the ceiling.

'Move! Out! Get out!' she began to shout.

The others turned blankly towards her.

'What's the smell?' sniffed Paddy.

'It's a fire, get up quick. Out, get out of here! Bloody well MOVE,' she screamed, grabbing Hannah who was half asleep and pulling her to her feet.

The boys were trying to lift the small television set.

'Bloody leave it, we've got to move.'

She pushed back through the open doorway into the kitchen. The whole wall was now alight, the lino was starting to curl and melt under them, a heavy black smell filled the kitchen. Back in the other part of the trailer, she grabbed a rug off the couch, lifted the sleeping Davey from the little cot and covered him with it.

She ran back towards the kitchen again. The whole floor was smothered in flames. The cupboards were alight. There was no way they could reach the caravan door. Sparks had run into the boys' room. In a few seconds the twins' mattress would be on fire. The pictures of motor bikes further up the wall had started to curl with the heat.

'We're stuck, Katie. We'll all be killed!' Brian was already beginning to cough and splutter. He'd always had a weak chest since he was a baby.

Time and time again Katie had heard that it was the smoke, the black greasy fumes of smoke from cushions and foam that killed people. They had only a minute or two to get out – already her eyes were beginning to weep. Davey in panic was trying to kick out of the rug; she wrapped it even tighter around him. At the other side of the living room the twins were twisting the screws on each side of the window. The curtains were starting to singe, the whole roof was beginning to crack and Katie could almost believe the floor supports were starting to sag.

'Help, help! Save us, help!'

The twins and Hannah were shouting and coughing, the noise of the TV drowning them out.

The boys tried to push the window. It was really stiff and would only open a fraction. Dad was meant to have oiled it and freed it up, but hadn't got around to it. Hannah was trying to squeeze through it, but was bent double, stuck.

'I'll be roasted alive. Mam! Mammy!' she screamed.

'We've got to break a window.' Katie's eyes scanned the room. It was hot, the fire was circling towards them. 'God help me.'

Then in the corner she spotted the iron golf stick. The twins had found it near a golf club where they searched for balls in the long grass. Mam had half-hidden it away from them in case they could do damage.

Hannah was back standing behind her, whimpering like a little puppy. The twins' faces looked scared. Brian was finding it really hard to breathe. Paddy was forcing him to stand and not sit down.

'Hannah, hold Davey. Don't drop him,' Katie ordered.

She raised the golf stick and began to beat at the glass. A line ran through it but it didn't crack. It took four goes before the glass shattered and she was able to push it out, but sharp pieces still stuck up. She dragged a chair over.

'Give me Davey.'

The child was livid with temper. It was a wonder the whole campsite hadn't heard the racket. The rug was off him and his kicks pounded against Katie's ribs.

Katie spread the doubled-over rug on top of the jagged window ledge.

'Get up, Hannah. Stand up on the chair.'

Hannah was up, quick as lightning. Her thin body clambering up over the window.

'The glass'll stick into me.'

'You'll be roasted otherwise. Stop messing, it's only a tiny jump,' Katie ordered her.

Hannah dithered, it wasn't much of a jump, but it suddenly seemed such a long way to the ground.

'Jump. Good girl, jump,' Katie pleaded.

Hannah wavered. The twins began to scream at her which seemed to break the spell. She jumped, and fell on her knees in the dirt, grazing them and her hands.

'Reach up, Hannah. Come on, look up at me.'

Hannah stood up. She was in shock.

'I'll pass down Davey to you,' Katie stated firmly.

'I won't be able to catch him, he'll fall. He'll break his back.'

'Shut up!'

'No! No! I can't.'

Already Katie was leaning over the uneven edge of the rug covering. Davey was bawling. His face was as red as a turkey cock and his curls were plastered to his head from the tears and sweat. Katie held him by his armpits. The chubby legs and feet flayed in the air. Hannah's skinny arms reached up to him. She was able to touch his ankles and halfway up his lower leg. He kicked and thrashed and squealed like a pig going to be slaughtered.

'I can't get him.'

'He's coming,' insisted Katie, grim-faced, hoping she was doing the right thing. Leaning over as far as she could she lowered Davey. She was conscious of a scraping, jagged feeling against her stomach, but she reached far forward. Hannah buckled under Davey's weight but managed to break his fall by landing on her bottom and back.

Davey was safe.

'Mam, help us, there's a fire!' Hannah screamed. Paddy had climbed over the windowsill and jumped down with ease, his face creased with worry and strain as he reached his arms towards his twin brother and helped pull him to safety.

From behind her Katie was conscious of a roar. She looked back. The three sides of the caravan were ablaze. Rivulets of fire ran over her head. Her heart slowed. She felt as if she had stopped breathing. The temptation was to stay rigid and still, to breathe in this strange heavy smell, to fill her lungs with it – so sticky and sweet – to close her eyes and let it cover her nose and mouth, to float away.

Her eyes felt so heavy ... maybe she should just shut them, it would be so easy.

'Kaaatie! My Kaaatie!'

A voice shrill and sharp and urgent pushed its way like a nail into her brain.

Mam was outside. She was standing shouting at

her. Ah Mam, don't be cross with me!

'Kaa-tie! My own Katie. Jump out!'

Tom was outside too. He had his arms around Mam's waist, like he was wrestling her and holding her back. As if in slow motion Katie could see Hannah, trying to keep hold of Davey. What was wrong with the twins? They were curled up in each other's arms, hugging each other. It was getting very hot and oh so dark.

She could see Mam's eyes. They were huge, like two pools of water.

'KATIE!

It was so loud and high, piercing her above the roar of the flames and the crackling of the wood all around her.

Mam wanted her. She jumped.

Chapter 7

DESTROYED

'Put your head down between your knees. Stay sitting, you're right winded.' Mam was fussing all about her.

She just couldn't stop herself shaking; it went through her whole body. Even her teeth were chattering. Someone put a blanket around her.

A heavy fog of thick black smoke engulfed their trailer, and a section of roof fell with a sickening crash.

Everyone ran back and forth with buckets and basins of water and flung them at the giant fire-dragon, but it only served to make the monster hiss and steam even more.

Auntie Brigid hurled a huge saucepan of stew towards the red centre of the flames; immediately the meat was singed and barbecued to lumps of charcoal, sizzling and disappearing in seconds. All the young cousins watched as their next day's dinner went up in smoke, trying to hide the selfish worry of what they would eat now.

Mam's face was like a ghost. Davey clung to her, terrified. She swayed on her feet.

'Move back. Get those kids back.' Old Man Casey was out, taking charge. He had only a pair of trousers on him.

'Move back, Missus. The whole roof will go in a minute.'

The heat was so intense that all the children in the field had reddened cheeks. Huge flames reached out like octopus tentacles to grab something else to burn. Like an arm brandishing a sword, a flash of flame suddenly streaked across the pole outside the door. The wooden step was on fire.

The blue horse stood out above the flames. But the fire soon began to grasp it and in a few seconds the paint blistered and burst. Horrified, Katie watched. The wooden shape seemed to swell – she could swear it was moving, bucking and kicking, trying to escape the flame. It was engulfed like a mini fireball.

She could almost hear its whinny as it burned.

With a whoosh there was another burst of fire. The whole roof had fallen in. There was no saving it now. Everyone just stopped. They stood still, hands hanging by their sides, mouths open.

Hannah stood beside Katie, her grimy hand on Katie's shoulder.

'My dollies ... my new black shoes ... my lovely pink cardigan – they're all still inside,' she wailed.

Katie turned round to face her. 'They're gone, Hannah, but we're safe. We all got out and that's all that matters. Things don't matter.' She said it as much for herself as for her little sister. The thought of the blue horse now gone was tearing her apart.

The twins were standing huddled together stroking Duffy. The young dog was doing her best to jump from the safety of their arms and join the crowd of other mongrels that roamed the campsite, all yapping and barking their heads off.

'Where's the fire brigade?'

One of the Caseys had run up to the houses to telephone. Two or three cars slowed up at the roadside as they spotted the flames and smoke, but there was no sign of the fire engine.

* * *

Sirens blaring and blue light flashing, the fire brigade appeared at last in the distance along the road. It turned off sharply and trundled across the dirt track towards them.

The chief fireman jumped out and took control immediately. One fire officer ran back up towards the road, looking for a hydrant. Once it was located, the long grey rubber hoses suddenly came to life as gallons of water were pushed through them, aimed at the fierce red shell of the caravan. A stench of ash and soot washed over the camp.

No one dared to speak. The firemen muttered sharp commands to each other. This was now their world, their fire and Katie was only an onlooker.

The fire suddenly seemed to give in. It was defeated, the battle over, every sign of light or brightness was extinguished, flattened out. Not even a spark of orange or yellow was left, only a mess of black and grey with dying breaths of steam coming off it. The ground was awash with filthy water that seeped everywhere. Katie's shoes were black and splashes of water stained her ankles and calves.

The trailer was destroyed, everything they had, gone. Katie tried to concentrate, to recreate the old-fashioned caravan with the pole and the blue horse outside it, but like a dream it had all vanished.

Two of the firemen, using long rods, moved among the debris, trying to discover what had caused this destruction.

The campsite held its breath. The children shifted uneasily; the women avoided each other's eyes. The flattened hoses were being rewound, the water squelching out of them whilst the silent inquisition went on.

The chief fireman had stopped. 'Where's the owner?' he shouted.

Katie watched as her mother came forward and walked towards him. He talked to her in low tones. Mam looked ashamed, like a child being punished. As if losing every stick they owned was not punishment enough.

'Had you checked the lights on the gas?'

She shook her head.

'You're damn lucky we don't need a fleet of ambulances here ...'

Two spots of colour flooded her mother's cheeks.

'Thanks be to God they're all safe. I'd die if any harm came to them.' She blessed herself with relief. 'I only went out for a short while and left the two older ones minding the others. I was right close by, almost next door.' Her explanation hung in the air. The fireman was too busy to listen.

'You couldn't be watching them every minute,'

she added lamely. The other women all nodded in agreement.

A fireman had taken out a first-aid kit and one by one he came around to them all. Over and over again he took Brian's pulse, checking his breathing and making him blow into some kind of contraption. He made Mam promise to take him to casualty in the hospital if he got any worse. He cleaned up the bad cuts on Hannah's leg, putting on tiny white strips of plaster. Davey was fine, apart from a bruise on his hip.

'Now, young lady, let me have a look at you.'

Katie felt like crying at the kindness of his voice.

'Any cuts or bruises?'

She shook her head.

'Come on, now, speak up.'

'I don't think so.' She felt herself all over. There was a long thin scrape on her stomach over her navel, where small dots of blood pushed through, but the cut wasn't deep. 'No, but my ankle is a bit sore.'

The fireman felt it.

'Probably from jumping out, but I don't think any bones are broken or any damage done. Probably will be a bit stiff and sore. Now, give a few coughs.'

Katie's chest and lungs were sore and ached.

'Come on now, good girl. I want you to watch me. Take a few good slow big deep breaths, the way I'm doing it.'

She watched him and copied him.

'Now, that's good, you're beginning to breathe more easily – and it's good for shock.'

Everything was packed away. The firemen had finished – the fire was over, so the firefighters could go home. But where would her family go? What would happen them now? These thoughts flooded Katie's mind as she watched the fire engine head back up to the road.

Chapter 8

ALL GONE

A heavy, gloomy silence fell on the campsite. Not one of the families would want to change places with Kathleen Connors and her brood. And they had brought bad luck to this place.

Auntie Brigid tried to be cheerful. 'A good strong cup of tea with plenty of sugar,' she announced.

Mam seemed to be in a trance. Auntie Brigid was fussing around them like a mother hen, trying to lead them towards her trailer. The rest of the travellers began to disperse back to their own vans. All had offered to help if they could.

It was agreed that Katie and Hannah and Mam and Davey would go to Auntie Brigid's trailer for the night.

Katie looked down at herself. A green sweatshirt with a cat on it and a T-shirt, her denim skirt and her two soaked shoes, that and her underwear were all she had in the world now. Just what she stood up in. She hadn't even a brush for her hair. The enormity of what had happened began to hit her.

'Come on, Kathleen, sit down, you poor thing, you're all done in. Girls, grab a place there beside your mother.' Auntie Brigid was trying to see if there was any water left in the place to make a cup of tea.

'Mam! Mammy! What will Da say when he sees the place?' asked Hannah.

Kathleen Connors did not reply. She just stared at the sugar bowl on the table as if it was a crystal ball and would show her what to do.

Katie knew that when her father appeared and saw the burnt-out caravan he would go crazy. This was the third trailer they'd had in the last few years. One was too small and another had rotted to bits after a very hard winter in a field that was as bad as a swamp. All winter long the rats had gnawed at the wood until you could hardly put a foot to the floor for fear you'd go through it. Saucepans caught the rain dropping from the leaking roof. Their last penny had gone to get this one ... Katie stopped herself. It was gone now – gone. Out of the blue her mother suddenly began to talk, talk, talk – non-stop.

'Everything is gone ... we're destroyed. We've nothing left, not a brass farthing ... we're ruined.'

'Hush, Kathleen, Kathleen.'

No matter what their aunt said Mam kept on talking. She began to list off everything that was gone, every piece of furniture, of ware, cooking stuff, clothes, family mementoes, getting more and more hysterical as she went on. 'And my wooden horse, the one my Granddaddy made – maybe it survived. You remember how long I have it, Brigid.'

Katie didn't have the heart to say she knew it was gone too, but was glad of the excuse to get away for a minute or two from the singsong voice, so strange and remote.

'Will I have a look for it, Mam?' Barely waiting for the reply she was outside.

The wooden pole had broken in three and lay blackened on the ground. The horse was definitely gone. Pools of water lay all around. Her cousins, the Faheys, were combing the debris to see if they could salvage anything. She hadn't the heart to join them. She spotted something vaguely familiar in one of the pools.

The horse! Quick as a wink Katie bent down. The wood had expanded and felt warm and all the paint had blistered off it – but if you knew it was meant to be a horse you might just recognise it.

'Oh horse, poor old horse.' She lifted it up and carried it into the other trailer to her mother.

'What's that bit of old wood you've got there?' demanded Auntie Brigid.

Her mother took it; she was left wordless now and her tears began to fall. The horse lay blackened and destroyed in front of her.

'Let her cry, girls, she needs to cry and get it out. I'll see to Davey. You sit there with your Mam.'

Hannah was scared and Katie had to admit that she was too. Mam just held their hands and cried and cried.

Before going to bed Tom and the twins came in to Mam and hugged her then left again quickly. A time like this and they couldn't even stay together as a family, thought Katie sadly. Where was Da?

Mam was exhausted and dozed off at last, with Hannah leaning against her. Uncle Mike kept coming in and out. He had been up to the town twice looking for his brother-in-law. All the cousins had been well warned to be good, and with the odd smack as a reminder, had gone to bed quietly. Everyone was waiting for Ned Connors to return. Finally the silence of the night was broken by the sound of a car as it bumped over the grass and came to a halt. Its lights lit up the spot where their trailer had once stood.

Katie heard an outburst of cursing outside, then the car door banged. In an instant her father was at the trailer door.

'God in heaven, Brigid! Where's Kathleen? Where's my kids?' he roared.

From her sleeping bag on the floor, Katie could see the telltale redness of his cheeks and smell the mixture of whiskey and cigarettes that explained his absence. Uncle Mike was talking to him and putting on the lights.

'Where's my wife? Is she all right?'

Mam stirred and rubbed her eyes, easing Hannah off her lap. Dad ran over and hugged her.

'Oh Kathleen, girl, thank God you're all right.'

''Tis all right, Ned. We've lost everything, but the family are all safe. Hannah and Katie and Davey are here and the boys are next door.'

'I'm fine, Da,' Katie murmured. He stepped over the others on the floor and hugged her too.

'God is good,' was all he said.

Relieved that her father was back, Katie at last felt that maybe it was safe to sleep.

He sat down beside Mam and she started to tell him the whole story of the fire over and over again.

Over and over again.

Over and over again it ran in Katie's mind too as she tried to sleep.

Chapter 9
THE OFFER

You couldn't swing a cat in the place. Auntie Brigid and Uncle Mike were doing their best to pass around bowls of porridge, but having five extra people in a trailer was just too much. The floor was covered with sleeping bags and blankets.

In the morning light Katie was ashamed of how dishevelled they looked. Maggie lent her a brush and a clean sweatshirt and pair of panties, but no one had her size shoes. Bridey and Hannah were much the same size and able to share clothes, and Tom and the twins had plenty of people to borrow from. One of the neighbours sent over a bag of things for Davey.

Once the curtains were opened it was very clear that everything they had had was gone. A cold hand of fear gripped Katie. Never in her life could she remember a time when things had been this bad. Mam had aged about ten years overnight. Da had a haunted look about him. The small box with their meagre savings had been discovered, but it had melted and the few notes inside it had curled away. Da paced up and down outside, kicking over bits of charred timber. They only had the old banger of a car left now. The twins appeared out of a caravan, along with Tom. They walked around the place, like three shadows following their father.

It was about eleven o'clock when a small car appeared. The woman driver drove right into the middle of the campsite and got out. In one hand she clutched a briefcase. She looked around quickly, then came and knocked at Brigid's door.

Auntie Brigid opened it. She obviously knew the woman and invited her in.

'Miss O'Gorman, this is my sister, Kathleen. Kathleen Connors. It's probably herself you've come to see today.'

'Yes, Brigid. I heard you and your family are fine at the moment. Let me introduce myself, Mrs Connors. I'm Annette O'Gorman. I'm a social worker for this area. I was informed last night of your predicament and I came straight away to see what we can do to help.'

Mam shook her hand. Katie could see she was still in a kind of trance. 'Mam! Mam! It's Miss O'Gorman, she's here to help us.'

'I heard, Katie.' Mam's voice was distant.

Auntie Brigid was embarrassed. 'Look, Miss O'Gorman, I'll leave you alone here for a while as I have to get to the shops.'

Katie coaxed Hannah and Davey outside. She just sat on the step as she hadn't one ounce of energy today to do anything. The social worker spoke gently to Mam, treating her like a child. She could see Mam was still dazed.

'Where are you going to live? You need somewhere to stay. Children need a roof over their heads.'

Mam nodded mutely. The social worker opened her case and spread her papers out on the table. 'We'll do our best to help you. First off, tell me the names and ages of your children.'

Mam reeled them off mechanically: Tom, Kathleen, Paddy, Brian, Hannah and baby David,' and the years they were born.

'What about any extra income coming in?'

Mam shook her head.

'Any savings, bank account, building societies?'

'Just a bit in a box, but it's gone now.' A sob escaped from Mam's throat. She sounded like she was going to break down crying.

'Take it easy, Mrs Connors – Kathleen – I'm here to help you. That's my job. Will you get another trailer or caravan?' Miss O'Gorman sounded calm and concerned.

'We haven't the money for one.'

'Would you think of settling?'

'We're travellers born and bred, it's our whole life,' Mam announced stubbornly. 'It would be very hard for us to settle.'

A heavy silence filled the air. Katie sat rigid with curiosity. She put her hands lightly over Davey's mouth to stop him gabbling so that she could hear.

'But you might have to settle, Kathleen.' The social worker said the words softly.

'How could we settle?' Mam whispered.

'It's very difficult to keep travelling forever and it's a hard and lonely road. Think of your children, their education, the chance of a job. Autumn and winter will soon be here. A roof over your heads is vital. I'm offering you a house for your family, Kathleen.'

'There's more to life than school and houses,' Mam protested.

Katie listened as the argument went back and forth. Her mother was wearing down. She had sent Hannah off to find Da and bring him here.

'Kathleen, it's a nice house, and other travellers have settled in the estate. It's near a school and shops, but I'll have to have a decision very soon. You've gone to the top of the list because of the emergency of your situation, having no home, but I can't hold this house forever for you, no more than a day or two.'

Katie watched as her father strode towards the trailer. He almost fell over her in his rush to get inside where he sat down beside Mam. His large hands ruffled his hair – he always did that when he was nervous.

'Ah Mr Connors, it's nice to meet you.' Miss O'Gorman held out her hand to greet him.

In a low voice Mam began to tell him of their conversation and about the offer. Miss O'Gorman butted in, telling him about the estate and one by one listing all the advantages of settling.

'I'm a travelling man.'

'Oh I know that, Mr Connors,' Miss O'Gorman agreed, 'but you're also a man with a wife and family, a husband and a father,' she added firmly.

'I'm a travelling man. I'll not live in any house!

If you government people want to help, give us a new caravan, that's all the help we need. We'll get back on our feet then and back on the road.'

'My department gives people homes not caravans, Mr Connors.' Miss O'Gorman pleaded her case as best she could.

Then suddenly, when Katie least expected it, Mam's voice: 'I've done with it, done with travelling, I want a proper roof over my head and four solid walls. The children to be safe and get a bit of an education. It's time to stop, Ned!'

Her father was stunned, then furious. 'No woman or children will tie me down. I'll not live in a house like settled people!'

'Well, I'm fed up with being different. I just want to be like the rest of them, I've had enough of it all. Miss O'Gorman, fill in those forms please and like a good girl do your best to get us a place in that housing estate.'

Ned Connors jumped to his feet and stormed out the door. Katie had never seen him in such a temper or so tense and angry. He went off and stood at the edge of the field, his back to them all. Katie looked at his broad, straight shoulders. He was a strong man, well respected and liked by all the travellers. She longed to run and fling her arms around him and say, Da, I love you, but her instincts told her this was a time he needed to be left alone. For all his kindness he was as stubborn as an old donkey and often there was no getting around him.

Mam and the social worker chatted away and finally came out to say goodbye. Mam's eyes flew towards the desolate, solitary figure.

'Mrs Connors, I'll send someone down later with some essentials for you and don't forget the vouchers I've given you.'

'Thank you, Miss, I'm very grateful for all your help. I'm sorry about himself shouting at you.'

'Don't mention it. You've all been through a huge shock, it's only to be expected.'

As soon as the car started up, a band of children ran along behind it, waving. Katie went over to her mother, who looked pale and tired.

'I heard you, Mam. Is it true we're really going to settle?'

Her mother nodded. She looked crushed.

'In a house?'

'Yes, lovey, if we keep our fingers crossed and are lucky.'

'Not a trailer or a van?'

'No! A proper house, with a bit of a garden to hang out washing, a bathroom and a toilet and three bedrooms and a fine big sitting-room with a kitchen behind it. There'll be shops and schools and all kind of things close by ...' Mam looked straight at Katie, searching her face and eyes for a reaction.

'Da'll never stand for it. He loves the road, he'll never settle,' Katie cried, unable to hide the fear and unease in her voice.

'Well, Katie, I've had enough. We haven't a

thing to our name now. The fire has done its worst and the fight has gone out of me. I'm not getting any younger. It's time I settled – that we all did. Wherever we are, your Da will always have a place, the door will be open for him.'

The door open for him! What the hell did that mean? Was Mam saying that Da might not go with them? They'd be on their own – she couldn't mean it. To leave the life they knew was bad enough, but the thought of Da not being there too ... a shiver ran through her.

'Are you okay, pet?' Mam looked at her.

'Yeah.'

'Are you sure?'

'Yes, Mam, don't be worrying.'

'Don't say anything to the others yet. There's nothing definite until we find out if we get the house. No point in upsetting them until we hear from Miss O'Gorman.'

Katie nodded and gave a sigh of relief. Maybe it wouldn't happen at all. Da might get the money for a trailer somewhere and things would be the same as always. Nothing was certain yet!

Chapter 10
LEAVING

Three black plastic bags – all they had in the world wrapped up in a few plastic bags. Katie was trying to stuff some clothes into one. Then she lifted them out to Uncle Mike's car. Maggie helped her squash them into the boot, which was full of old car batteries and junk. The twins were hanging around the car door. They didn't look themselves. They were too neat and too tidy and far too quiet. They're scared too, Katie guessed.

Mam and Auntie Brigid were talking. The last few days had been a terrible strain on both families.

'Too many children in too small a space,' Brigid said consolingly. They were all getting on each other's nerves. Even Maggie and herself had had a fight. Katie spilled some tea on a white jumper of Maggie's and her cousin called her a clumsy cow and told her to wash it straight away. But they had made it up.

Da disappeared off every day, hoping something would turn up, but he had no luck. He slept in the car at night.

Mam tried again and again to talk to him, but he wouldn't listen.

'We can go back on the road if you don't like the house, I promise, Ned. Just give it a try. We need a roof over our heads for the winter.'

'I don't want a house. I'll not go.'

'You have no choice, we all have no choice.'

'There is a choice. No one in a big city office will decide where my children grow up or how they live!'

* * *

They had made a kind of tent in the field and the boys slept in it. Mam had brought out bread and marmalade to them for their breakfast. Da sat cross-legged with them.

'It's this morning, Ned!'

Da kept eating the bread and said nothing.

'We'll get the keys of the house today, Ned. Number 167 Ashfield Drive will be ours.'

He just ignored her.

'You've got to come and see it, Ned. I can't do it all on my own.'

'I'm busy today. You do what you want.' He got up and waving the car keys in his hand jumped into the old Ford and took off, sending scuds of dust into the early morning air.

'Well, that's it!' said Mam, a strange emptiness in her voice, as she watched him drive off. 'You lot get up and get tidied, there's plenty of work to be done. Fold up that tent and pack up!'

Katie felt as if she was in a dream.

Mam seemed like a stranger, her face set like a mask. She put Katie in charge of Davey. He was very fractious, knowing something was up, and he was fretting and upset. Katie tried to play with him but her mind wasn't on it at all. Miss O'Gorman arrived at about half-past eleven.

'Mrs Connors, there's been a bit of a change of plan. We have to delay moving you into the house until later on today.'

'Is there a problem about it?' Mam queried.

'No ... well ... '

'What is it?'

'Well ... actually, the house is fine, the men went out to check that everything was in order this morning. But we have a little bit of a problem all right.'

'What sort of problem?'

'Well ... well ... actually one or two of the neighbours are objecting to you moving in.'

'What do you mean, objecting?'

'They're walking up and down outside on the road.'

'You mean it's a protest, or a march? Is that it? I've heard about that from other travellers. People shouting and screaming at you, telling you you're not wanted. My God, are they the kind of neighbours we're going to have?'

Katie felt scared. 'We won't go, Mam, we'll stay here. Da'll sort something out. Tell them to keep their stinking, rotten house. We don't want it.'

'Maybe Katie's right. Maybe we shouldn't go if we're not wanted there.' Mam was on the verge of tears.

'No! No! Mrs Connors, it's not that, it's not you personally they're objecting to, it's just travellers in general, settling, being given a house. They think it might bring trouble to their area.'

'We'll bring no trouble nor give no trouble, did you tell them that?'

'I did. I talked to some of them myself. Some of it is that they have children and relations waiting a long time for a house and they feel you've jumped the queue, so to speak.'

'But we were never in a queue.'

'Yes, yes, I know that. And we have to make provision for emergency housing, all state agencies have to. Try not to let it bother you.'

'What do we do now?'

'I think it's wise to wait until after seven o'clock. Hopefully they'll have got fed up and gone home by then.'

Mam seemed deflated. A worried frown creased her face. Katie had sense enough not to try and talk about what was going on.

Auntie Brigid had made a huge meal for them all – you'd nearly think it was going to be their last meal ever! And there was a big sponge cake with mandarin oranges on the top for dessert, a real treat.

Six o'clock came, then seven, and there was still no sign of Da.

*　　　*　　　*

'Brigid, how can I ever thank you for being so good to us?' Mam and Auntie Brigid hugged each other as if they were going to be separated for ever.

'When I get a chance in a week or so I'll come over to see the place and we'll have a chat.'

Mam nodded dumbly.

Hannah and Bridey were running around the field for the last time. Katie picked up Davey and stood in the centre of it all, the only world she'd ever known. The trailers and vans and the blackened site where their home had been. She glanced at the spot where Francis's caravan had been, and the goats. Nan Maguire had been right. This wasn't a lucky place. Katie knew in her heart that once they left, it would be only a matter of a few days and the rest of them would be gone too. In a few weeks' time the grass would be high again. When they left this time a huge gulf would divide the Connors family from the rest of the travellers, separating those in houses and those on the road. They had lost so much already and they would be different now from their kinfolk and family.

Uncle Mike was getting impatient. Tom had caught Duffy and was sitting in the back of the car, trying to stop the dog whining to get out.

'Into the car, come on, I haven't all evening,' shouted Uncle Mike.

Hannah and the twins got in and sat staring out. The other children had run off and were playing down behind the caravans and already seemed to have forgotten their existence.

Mam held two battered saucepans in her hand and a brand new frying pan still in its wrapper, a present from the Caseys. She kept looking up towards the roadway, hoping Da would appear.

'Where's Da?' whinged Brian. 'I won't go to the

new house without Da!'

'He's got a bit of business,' Mam answered.

'But where is he? He should be here by now.'

'He had to go to Galway,' Mam answered firmly. 'Now be good or he'll be right cross with you when he does see you.'

Katie squeezed in beside her brothers and took Davey on her lap.

Mam and Brigid were whispering to each other. Brigid shrugged her shoulders. 'He'll turn up. Don't fret, Kathleen, they're his kids too.'

Mam got in. Uncle Mike started the engine. He beeped the horn and everyone clustered around and called goodbye and good luck.

Katie was glad that Francis and his grandmother were not here. She could never have said goodbye without crying if he was still there. Maggie flung a few sweets in at them through the open window. Even Duffy managed to grab one and swallowed it in one gulp, still wrapped in its paper.

Katie half-expected Da to pull up in the car and jump out to say he'd got a new trailer and found a great place to camp. Time was running out. But he didn't ... Time was frozen still.

She could hear the horn beeping and felt the motion as the car lurched forward. The others were waving goodbye. Mam stared straight ahead and didn't say a word. Katie knew it was hopeless. She pulled Davey closer.

'This little piggy went to market,' she said mechanically, lifting up one little bare toe after another. She had no interest in looking out the window, she didn't give a toss about where they were going. A part of her was dead.

They were leaving the life they knew, giving up the road, giving up freedom.

Chapter 11

NUMBER 167

Ashfield estate was about twelve miles away, a huge, sprawling mass of houses built outside a large town. It was a late August evening, still bright when they arrived and lots of kids were playing in the roads, kicking footballs and hitting little multicoloured balls with tennis racquets. Bikesof every size wove in and out and little girls pushed prams with dolls.

'Plenty of kids anyway,' Uncle Mike laughed. They passed row after row of houses, one the same as the next. Bare-looking trees pushed their way up through concrete paths and tired-looking grass added a hint of green in places. It was a huge estate, like a big grey maze that once you entered you'd never find your way out.

The twins both sat up.

'Is this Ashfield, Mam?' asked Brian.

'Yes, pet, this is it, but we have to find our road.'

'Doesn't look too bad,' announced Paddy.

Katie sighed. Trust the twins. Once they had a ball and a few people to kick it around with, they were happy. From the corner of her eye she spotted groups of girls here and there, sitting on garden walls or just standing around, all in denims. They stared at the car, they stared at her. Some giggled.

'More tinkers!' she heard one of them jeer.

Houses, houses, and every one of them the same.

It was all so drab-looking. Mother of God, how would they even know which one was meant to be theirs? Three windows and a front door. Most of them hadn't even a number.

'Are you sure you have the right address?' Uncle Mike was driving up and down the roads, certain that they were passing houses they had seen already.

At last Mam recognised Miss O'Gorman's car and shouted, 'Stop, Mike, it's somewhere here, slow down.'

'Thanks be to God,' said their uncle, braking and swinging the car around suddenly, knocking the front wheel off the kerb.

'Look there, it's Miss O'Gorman, Mam!' Hannah was waving at the social worker who was standing at the front door.

A middle-aged man, two women and a teenage boy marched up and down in front of number 167. They held a piece of cardboad on a stick. 'No More Tinkers' was printed on it with black marker.

'Who are those people, Mam?' asked Brian.

'I suppose they must be the protesters, your new neighbours,' said Uncle Mike.

Everybody seemed to stop and turn and stare into the car.

'Come on in, Mrs Connors.' Miss O'Gorman came running down the path to the gate. She ignored the hostile group and urged Mam and the children out of the car.

'No more timkers here!' shouted the group of protesters. 'Tinkers out!'

'Don't take any notice of them,' Miss O'Gorman said and she marched straight up to the front door, turned the key and swung it open. 'Come on in,' she called, beckoning them forward.

They all stood on the path and kept their eyes down, then slowly made their way to the door avoiding the noisy group. Some of the children playing had stopped to watch. Katie's face burned scarlet and she clutched Hannah's hand tightly.

The house looked like all the others except maybe a bit worse. The driveway was cracked and bits of moss grew up through it. The hall door was painted a cream colour but was peeling.

'It's not too bad, is it?' said Mam anxiously.

'Kathleen, it's grand, a right little palace. Well built and solid, by the look of it,' her brother-in-law answered her, and then moved off to get their stuff from his car.

'Well, Katie and Hannah, Tom and Paddy and Brian, aren't you coming in to look at your new home?' Miss O'Gorman smiled at them.

Katie still held Hannah's hand. 'Mam, come on, you go first,' she urged. It was Mam's place to take the first step. It was too important, only Mam should do it.

Mam walked through the door and the rest of them followed one by one. Mam's eyes darted around nervously, taking in the whole place.

'Well, Kathleen! What do you think?' Miss O'Gorman was smiling from ear to ear.

Mam was barely able to talk.

'It's lovely, Miss, we'll make it a right proper home,' Katie filled in.

The shouting was still going on outside, but soon Miss O'Gorman closed the door.

'Don't worry about them,' she said, 'they've lost their steam and they'll go off home soon, you'll see. I'm sure they'll leave you alone after this – they've made their protest. Anyway, the house is yours now and they can't do a thing about it.'

They stood in the living-room where there was a big window that looked out on the roadway and at the houses directly across. Down the small hall-way was a kitchen with a window and a door leading to the back garden, a small square of con-crete and grass where a whirly washing line lay spreadeagled and broken. The other room was smaller and darker and it was totally empty, with bare wooden floorboards.

The twins began to run around, the dog follow-ing them as they chased in and out of the rooms shouting. Duffy was demented with excitement and ran around in circles in a frenzy of running and yelping. Tom stood awkward and embar-rassed. He didn't know where to go or what to do so he went out to help Uncle Mike. Hannah was jumping up and down. 'My house, my house, my house,' she sang in a strange secret voice.

Katie looked around. It was smaller than she'd imagined and everything was painted brown or beige. The place needed a good clean out. She noticed cigarette burns on the lino in the kitchen.

'It's massive,' shouted Brian.

He raced up the stairs and the thump and clatter of feet came from the bare floorboards above Katie's head.

'Come and see the bedrooms and the bathroom, Katie,' Hannah shouted down at her.

Mam was chatting to Miss O'Gorman who was busy explaining the electricity meter and the gas meter and showing her how to heat water with the immersion. She pointed out the different keys and told Mam what day the bin men came and where the shops were.

'I know it's very empty, Kathleen, but tomorrow we'll organise beds and some furniture and a few bits and pieces, maybe a rug or two ...'

'I'll be fine, Miss, we'll fix it up and make it comfy, just wait and see.'

'Will you stay the night then or come back tomorrow?'

'No, we've enough to do us. Brigid and Mike gave us a loan of some sleeping bags and cushions. We'll make do – this is our place now and we're here to stay,' Mam announced firmly.

Katie smiled to herself and went to join the others upstairs. The big bedroom would be for Mam and Da and Davey. She was sure that Da would join them in time. Evening sunlight flooded the room. A bare bulb hung from a wire in the ceiling and swung backwards and forwards. A long mirror was screwed onto the wall. Katie stared at the reflection. The girl who stared back at her looked strange. She was able to see her whole self, the long skinny legs with the bumpy knees and the shortish body. Maggie's shirt was a bit too loose and made her look bigger than she really was. Her skin was fair and summertime had painted a multitude of light brown freckles all over her arms and shoulders and face. Her hair was far too thick and red, and it escaped from the navy hairband and strayed all around her. She pulled a face, then straightened herself.

'Hi, Kathleen Connors! Welcome to your new home,' she mimicked in a posh voice.

'Talking to yourself, Katie, you know what they say!' She blushed and caught sight of Tom who came and stood behind her. He was only a little bit taller than her but was of a much more sturdy build. His young face was serious and so like Da's.

'Do you think it'll change us?' Katie wondered.

He shrugged. 'Maybe.'

'Will you change, Tom?'

'I don't know if I can change, if it's that easy.'

'But we have a house now.'

'I know, but we're still travellers born and bred.'

'We always will be,' she agreed.

'Yeah, but people are always trying to change people into something else, make them more brainy, make them stronger, make them thinner, better-looking, make them richer, make them kinder, make them the opposite of what they are. I'm not sure if I can or if I want to change, or for that matter if I want to stay in a house!'

'It's a nice house, we're lucky to get one.'

'Yeah, but maybe I really am like Da and can't settle. I wanted to stay with him but no one bothered to ask what I wanted.'

'Kaa-tie!' Hannah was calling her.

She stared back into the mirror. Her eyes locked with those of her brother. Tom never said much but in those few seconds she could see pain and bewilderment and confusion. A little boy lost, a boy who wasn't a man yet, but a kind of a man who wished he was still a boy.

Abruptly he turned and went in to join the twins in the bedroom. She followed silently. A rather wrecked-looking bunk frame was still attached to the walls. The wood had been painted scarlet and black by the last tenants, yet it would look all right once new mattresses were got.

'I'll put my bed opposite you lot,' grunted Tom, throwing a navy sleeping bag on the floor to mark out his spot straight away.

Hannah grabbed Katie and drew her into the small bedroom. It was tiny.

'We'll need bunks, Katie, but isn't it lovely?'

The walls were bare but at some stage had been painted pink, someone – probably the last girl to sleep in the room – had covered the door with stickers and transfers. The small square window looked out at the back of the house, straight at the house behind, at walls and windows, more walls and more windows. There wasn't even a bit of a curtain. Katie spied a girl standing in a kitchen, then a man cutting bread, making sandwiches. Everybody could see everybody else. Through the gaps between the houses, in the far distance beneath the line of evening cloud she could see the gentle curving green, smudged with the darker green of trees. It was the mountains – the Dublin Mountains. She thought of Da; he always liked the mountains. If you stared really hard you could almost imagine you could touch them.

'Ma, come up to the wee room. I can see the mountains.'

'Later, pet.'

'Bye, everyone!' It was Miss O'Gorman leaving. 'I'll see you tomorrow morning again.' The front door closed and Katie heard the sound of the engine starting. Uncle Mike and Mam came in and walked around the house.

He admired every bit of the place.

'Honest to God, woman, if Brigid sees this I won't get a bit of peace.'

'Oh Mike … I …'

'I'm only joking, girl, you've done right well for yourself getting this place. I'll tell Ned all about it, but, well, you know how he is, it'll take him time to come round.'

Uncle Mike hugged them all. He gave them a fifty-pence piece each and told them it was for sweets in the local shop and to get something small for Davey too. They stood at the door and waved goodbye as he drove off back down the road. The protesters had gone at last and they ignored the stares of the neighbours and went back inside and closed the door.

Mam was so excited despite being tired. She had found an old bag with a bit of coal out in the back garden and also a half block of turf briquettes. Tom brought them in.

'I know it's still summer but the night is getting cool,' Mam said. ' Will I light the fire?' It seemed to take ages but eventually it began to catch.

There were no curtains on any of the windows. Tom and Katie went into the kitchen. There was an old cooker there, which needed a huge amount of cleaning, and one small cupboard attached to the wall. They took out a full sliced pan and made plateful after plateful of toast. Katie scraped each slice with butter quickly so it would melt straight away. They boiled water in a saucepan and made mugs of tea. Then they all sat crosslegged around the fire sipping the tea, full of milk and sugar, trying to relax. Katie's only regret was that Da wasn't there amongst them all. Mam chatted and told them about the tiny wagon she had grown up in. What would Grandma Whelan say if she saw this fine big house!

Paddy and Brian were yawning like mad, their cheeks flushed with sleep.

'Come on, I think it's time for bed, everyone,' Mam declared.

The light switch in the boys' room didn't work, so they clambered in the dark into the bunks despite having no mattresses, and pulled a blanket around themselves. Tom zipped up his sleeping bag. Uncle Mike had given him a radio when he left the site and Tom turned it on really low. Mam left them the torch.

Hannah and Katie had two pillows, a light blanket to lie on and a multicoloured nylon sleeping bag which they used as a quilt.

Katie could hear the twins giggling and then she heard Tom turning off his radio. It was a funny thing, but houses seemed to be full of strange noises – water running through a pipe overhead, creaking sounds from the roof, and every time someone moved on the floorboards she could hear it.

Mam was moving around downstairs. She seemed very far away. Even Tom and the twins were a long way off. She rolled to one side. Hannah was out for the count and her mouth hung open. She murmured the odd time in her sleep and gradually Katie could feel herself slipping ... there was something strange, something missing ... what was it? Then it came to her – it was standing still and it looked almost wooden. It raised its long neck and tossed its mane, which caught the breeze. It stared at her, then it began to run, to gallop. They were near the slope of a mountain – it cantered and whinnied and drew itself up on its back legs. It shook its head back and forth and its huge eyes never left her face. It wanted all her attention. The blue horse was calling to her. It was so big. She walked towards it, making soft little sounds, ready to pat it, to stroke it, to calm it down.

Its large hooves pushed backwards – it swished its blue tail and snorted; this was no ordinary horse. It could see into her very soul. The horse was lost, it was scared, it was angry. The nearer she got the more her sense of danger was alerted. The horse might kick her! It reared up.

She was reaching out to touch it, to pat it, when a roll of hooves took it off away from her. It was going further and further away ... the blue horse was going ... with a jolt she sat up. She felt empty, disorientated. The room was so strange.

'Mam! Mam!'

She sat up. Honest to God, she was as bad as the twins or Hannah, waking up with a nightmare.

She rubbed her eyes. She felt an overwhelming desire to be with her mother, to reassure herself that Mam was in the house. Slipping from under the sleeping bag she went down the wooden stairs trying not to make too much noise.

Mam was sitting in front of the fireplace staring at the dying flames. Near her, Davey's head rested on a cushion and he was snugly wrapped in two rugs. Mam didn't seem to hear her. She tiptoed up and whispered. 'Mam! Mam, I had a bad dream.'

'It's all right, pet, sit down here beside me and pull this blanket over you. It's just that everything is so strange. There have been a lot of changes in a few short days. You're worried about it, that's all.'

Katie nodded.

Mam put her arms around Katie.

'I'm worried too. I hope we've done the right thing. I'm worried about your Da – there's a lot that I –'

They were interrupted by the arrival of one sleepy twin after the other. They had their sleeping bags and blankets and without any fuss settled themselves in front of the fireplace.

'Can't sleep in that room,' Paddy declared, his eyes closing again almost immediately. Katie waited to see if Mam would send them back upstairs, but she just seemed to accept that they needed to be with her. About fifteen minutes later Hannah appeared, almost falling down the strange stairs with the sleeping bag wrapped cocoon-like around her. She was upset and crying.

'I thought you'd all gone off and left me, I called your names. Why didn't you come?'

'Hannah, come over here to me – go easy or you'll wake Davey up.'

Katie was moved further away. Hannah pushed her head against Mam and curled into her, her tears and upset fading away. A stab of jealousy stung Katie; the younger you were the more love you got.

There was a sense of reassurance with them all gathered in the small living-room. Tom's snores rumbled away upstairs, but the rest of them took comfort from each other and finally relaxed. Things felt more normal now. Maybe they'd be able to sleep within four walls and under a black tiled roof after all.

Chapter 12
DOOR-TO-DOOR

With every day that passed Katie began to feel that number 167 was home – well, maybe!

Miss O'Gorman took Mam over to a big storage depot. Beds and blankets, a small fridge that made a funny sound when you opened the door, a green and grey checked couch and wobbly armchair were among the things delivered the next morning. Everything was second-hand, someone else didn't want them, but they did the Connors family just fine. The house didn't seem as empty as it had the first night. There was a discount shop down in the town and Mam went there to get plates and cups and bowls and a silver-coloured kettle and a teapot.

They still had no curtains. The morning sun streamed in so early every day that they were first up in the neighbourhood. It was funny watching out the window as other people came downstairs in dressing gowns and ate breakfast and got ready for their day.

Next door a woman called Mrs Dunne lived with her son and daughter. Her eldest girl was married and brought two grandchildren to see her every weekend. Mrs Dunne's husband had died of a heart attack two years ago.

Katie noticed that at first Mrs Dunne would avoid being outside if any of them were around.

She seemed embarrassed to talk to them – even to say hello!

It was Duffy constantly pushing her nose through the back fence that got Mrs Dunne talking. She liked dogs and used to drop scraps of food over the fence to Duffy – bits of meat and left-over chicken. Maybe she thought they didn't feed her. Anyway, because of Duffy, she and Mam began to chat. She had lots of good advice to give Mam about training dogs and bringing them up. Mam would nod and listen, and try to hide her knowing smiles.

On the other side were the Foxes. They were well named, Katie decided, as they were a sly, cunning lot, always coming and going. They barely spoke and made it clear they had objected to having travellers as neighbours. A large rain-soaked piece of white cardboard still lay flung on the grass in their cluttered back garden. 'Keep Out The Tinkers' it said. Day by day the message was slowly being washed away.

Mrs Fox was a real gossip, always watching out the windows to see what they were at. Paddy and Brian would pull faces when they spotted her.

'Leave the poor soul alone,' scolded Mam. 'I think she's lonely, that's why she's so interested in other people's lives.'

Mam was far too soft.

Paddy and Brian had taken to Ashfield as easy as pie. The road seemed crammed with young fellows their own age and as soon as they were up in the morning they ran out to join the army of pals that kicked ball and played chasing out in the road.

But Hannah was different. Katie was sick of telling her to go out, but still she would not venture beyond the front wall. Katie lost her temper with her one day.

'Hannah, would you go out and play! Look at her, Mam.'

There she was sitting on the front wall, swinging her feet, her eyes wide, humming softly to herself. A crowd of girls about her own age, seven and eight, would set up a game deliberately near her only a house or two up, but never ask her to play. Hannah would watch them intently and Katie knew she was secretly keeping score and longing to join them. If a ball came near her she would jump down and try to grab it, and then stand with it in her hand, hoping they'd ask her to play.

'Give us back our ball,' was all they'd shout. Hannah would toss it back, but there was still no sign of them asking her to join in.

'Don't be bothered with them, Hannah,' urged Katie. 'Pretend you don't care, and ignore them.'

But her little sister wouldn't. She seemed content to sit on the wall and watch.

The kids in the estate were a funny lot. Some were fairly friendly, but others stared as if you were from outer space. Sometimes during the day the doorbell would ring and when they went to answer it there was no one there.

'Just kids messing,' Mam said, but it did worry Katie a bit. Sometimes it happened late at night, around midnight or even later. That was too late to be 'just kids'.

Katie and Tom both found notes pushed through the letterbox. Luckily Mam couldn't read the messages:

> *Get out filthy tinkers.*
> *Knackers go back on the road.*
> *You are not welcome here.*
> *Go away or there will be trouble.*

The writing and the paper was always different but the basic message was the same – go away.

Tom was angry about it and had all kinds of plans to try and catch whoever did it. Katie just hoped it would stop, and they both agreed not to let Mam know about it. She had enough on her plate to deal with.

*   *   *

'Will you come door-to-door with me?' Mam asked a few days after they moved in. They took Hannah, and Davey in the buggy, and went to an estate twenty minutes away on the bus. Mam knocked on the doors.

'Would you have a bit of help, Missus? I've just moved in with the family to a new house. Any spare sheets or towels or household goods would be very welcome.'

Some banged their doors shut, and others chatted and were quite friendly. After two hours there was barely enough space for Davey to sit in the buggy, and both Hannah and Katie held an assortment of plastic bags. Mam held her head high walking back down to the main road. 'No harm in getting what others don't want,' she declared. Later that night she was all excited, sorting out the odds and ends to see what they could use. She draped a huge white sheet over the living-room window and hung curtains on two of the upstairs windows. The begging had certainly been worthwhile.

'Wait till Brigid sees the place. I'm right proud of it,' beamed Mam.

'When will Da see it?' asked Hannah before Katie could stop her.

'Soon, pet. Any day now, that's what I'm hoping.'

A week later Katie was thrilled to see Maggie and Bridey and her aunt arrive for a visit.

'We left the wild ones back home,' joked Auntie Brigid.

Home – it had changed again. They were living in a different field now, practically on the side of the road.

'Not as nice at all,' whispered Maggie. 'I wish we had a place like this, we'd be rightly set up then.'

Hannah was delighted to have Bridey for company and took her out to sit on the wall to show off that she had a friend too.

Mam was busy trying to get information about Da and his whereabouts.

'You must have seen him, Brigid? Is he all right? Was he asking after us? Do you know where he is?'

'He's in Cork, Kathleen.'

'You mean to tell me he's down at the other end of the country!'

They tried to chat and laugh, and pass it off, but Katie knew that as far as Mam was concerned, all the good was gone from the visit.

Chapter 13

SCHOOL

'Summer's coming to an end,' announced Mam next morning. 'We must sort out about school.' She ordered them all to have a bath, wash their hair and dress in the best clean clothes they had.

'We'll go down to the schools and see what's what, so hurry up the lot of you.'

Tom lay splayed out on his bed and would not budge. 'I'm not going, Mam. I'm finished with schooling.' At almost fifteen, he had his mind made up.

'There might be some kind of course or centre for you to go to.'

'Mam, let me be. All last year I worked with Da. I can't go back to desks and books now. I'm done with it.'

'But what'll you do then, son? Please, just come with us,' she pleaded.

'No, you go on. I'll stay home. I've things to think about.'

He was adamant and would not move.

The rest of them pulled the hall door closed behind them and set off down the road.

Saint John's National School was only about ten minutes' walk away. It was a low grey building with green-painted iron railings all around. It served most of Ashfield and the other big estates nearby.

The caretaker opened the door and showed them all into a large waiting area with wooden benches. The boys and Hannah began to play a form of hopscotch on the tiled floor. It was so weird and spooky being in a school during holidays; it felt hollow and any noise echoed around the empty corridors and rooms.

Mr Searson, the headmaster, came out to meet them and brought Mam into his office. Katie was left to mind the others. It took about twenty minutes for Mam to reappear, then Paddy and Brian and Hannah had to go into the office and the headmaster talked to each of them and gave them a sheet of paper to fill in which took another half-hour. Katie pushed Davey up and down the corridors to pass the time. They all seemed very quiet when they came back and Paddy whispered that it was 'real hard'. The caretaker made a cup of tea for Mam. She was very nervous. The clock ticked on and on.

Finally Mr Searson brought them all into his office.'Well, Mrs Connors, they have all done the tests I've given them, difficult enough if you have been in and out of schools too often.'

Mam reddened.

'As I told you our classes are very large here, we cover a wide catchment area, and there are very few places ... however, that said, I can only offer one place.'

Katie looked anxiously at Hannah, whose eyes were wide, full of hope.

'One of the boys – Brian, isn't it?' he added.

Katie gasped. Brian! Only him? How could it be?

'His learning skills are just about right for his age and his marks are very good; some problems with spellings but we do have a remedial teacher here to help with things like that.' The man was staring at Brian with a smile on his face.

'But what about Paddy? The twins have never been separated.' Mam looked at Paddy who had slumped in the chair as if an unknown assailant had suddenly pounded him in the guts. 'What class will Paddy be in, or Hannah?'

'Well that's it, that's my problem, Mrs Connors, they won't be in any class. I'm full up. Paddy, even if I had a place, would be about two classes behind Brian. They would not be together anyway. He needs to work a lot harder to catch up. I don't know if putting him in a big class and letting him fall behind would be doing him any favours. Hannah, well!' He turned to Hannah. 'Do you understand about reading at all, Hannah?'

The little girl looked scared out of her wits, her blue eyes huge like an animal caught in a trap. Katie felt like hitting the middle-aged greying man in his striped suit for the pain he was causing her.

'Come on, don't be afraid to say what you feel.'

'I don't understand it, not any of it. The words all have strange sounds and when they're all spread out on a page it's like a big puzzle and I'm meant to make sense of it. Most of the time I can't make any sense of it. I'm not very good, am I?' With a wobble in her voice she raised her head and stared straight at the man.

'Did you go to school at all?' Mr Searson asked gently.

'Indeed they did, Mr Searson. Hannah and all of them have been in schools all over the place. Wherever we moved to we always tried to get them into a school or there would be someone to take a few of them and teach them their letters or what they needed to know to get them ready for their communion. We did our best for them.'

'I know, Mrs Connors. Life on the road is hard, and moving around for no matter what reason or what the cause is not the best thing for a child's education.'

'We're travellers, that's our life,' Mam interjected stubbornly.

'Yes, well, taking that into account I'd like to make a suggestion. We're very lucky that there's a special school for travellers on the far side of town. The children are collected by bus. It's a good school, and Hannah and Paddy would both do well there and hopefully be able to re-learn the basics.'

'But the twins have never been split up. They go everywhere, do everything together. I'd hoped the three of them would go to the same school, the one nearby.' Mam was staring at him.

'Look, Mrs Connors, it's the best I can do. I have an enormous school to run here. None of my teachers has the time to teach Hannah on her own, the time has to be shared between thirty-five other children too. I have to be fair to everyone!' He stopped for a moment considering an idea. 'Maybe if you or your husband could do a bit of reading work with them?'

Mam was silent for a second.

'Mr Searson, I'm on my own at the moment and ... well ... I can't read nor write myself.'

The headmaster was embarrassed and began to trip over himself trying to apologise.

'I'll help her, I'll help them both,' Katie volunteered. 'I'm good at reading.'

'Now that's the idea,' Mr Searson smiled. 'Where do you go to school?'

'Nowhere.'

'There's a very good Community School close by. You might consider it. Otherwise there's a convent school for girls in the centre of town.'

'I'll think about it,' muttered Katie, 'nothing's been decided yet!'

'Well, Mrs Connors, it's lovely to meet you and your family. Think about Brian and let me know by the end of the week.'

'I'll think about it, Mr Searson.' Mam was standing up to go. 'Thank you for your time.'

They left the school a silent bunch. In a few weeks' time the yard would be crowded and noisy with children and Katie couldn't help but wonder would Brian be one of them.

'Will we go to the Community School today, pet?' Mam asked her. 'Are you in the mood for it?'

'Not today, Mam. I'm not sure about school.'

'Well, tomorrow's another day. Anyway, I'll find out from Miss O'Gorman about it and what she thinks I should do. I wish your Da was here ... just to talk to ...'

Katie nodded.

'But no point in wishing, I've given up on that.'

'Me too,' whispered Katie, watching the grey drabness of the road.

Chapter 14

SEPTEMBER

Mam talked to one or two of the neighbours and to Miss O'Gorman to get advice about school. The social worker agreed that James Searson was a fair and sensible man. Twins were often split up so maybe it would be for the best. She gave Katie the application forms for the Community School but Katie wasn't that much bothered. Tom was staying home, maybe she would too.

The first day of September was on top of them before they knew it. Brian was all excited and Miss O'Gorman surprised him with a vivid blue school-bag that strapped over his shoulders and a grey school jumper and tie. Paddy went off into the bedroom in a huff.

When Mam walked with Brian down to the national school, half the neighbourhood seemed to be heading in the same direction. Brian was very nervous, but relaxed a bit when some of his football pals fell into step with him.

Mam came back almost sick with worry, but praying that Brian would be okay.

Half-an-hour later a red and grey bus stopped almost outside the door. The driver, a burly red-faced man, got out holding a list in his hands. Paddy and Hannah were the only two from their road going.

Mam and Katie went out to the bus with them.

About eight other children were on it already. Hannah was crying a bit and showing all the signs of getting herself in a right state. Mam was trying to hurry her along.

'Come on, I haven't got all morning, Missus,' said the driver. 'Tell her to make up her mind if she's coming or going. I have another twenty at least to pick up.'

Hannah looked over at Katie beseechingly. 'Katie, come with me, please.'

Katie hesitated. She had barely washed herself this morning she had been so busy getting the rest of them ready. She had brushed Hannah's hair and picked out two green clips, one for each side.

'First day is it?' the driver said, a little more kindly. 'The older girl can come if she wants to, but she'll have to walk back.'

'Please, please, Katie. I want you to see our school. Please come, just this morning.'

Mam nodded in agreement and Katie jumped up and grabbed a seat beside Hannah. Hannah always got her own way in the end, where Katie was concerned.

The bus journey was fairly long. They turned back onto the main road and then into a neighbouring estate, where about ten young travellers got on. They seemed to know the other children on the bus and just ignored the newcomers. The bus called to a halting site and seven more youngsters got on, their parents waving goodbye from the three trailers parked on the concrete yard. One of the boys, a cheeky fellow with a mop of blond curls pushed in beside Paddy and was trying to chat to him. The last call was to a roadside. Behind a clump of hedgerow, a caravan roof peeped through, then two little girls appeared out of nowhere and climbed up on the bus.

The bus finally turned off the main roads and headed up a bumpy sideroad. Two or three times the driver shouted to the kids to sit down. 'Any trouble on the bus and that'll be the end of it,' he kept threatening. 'I'm watching you all.'

Katie hoped she would remember the way back to the main road. As they turned around the corner she caught a first glimpse of the neat, whitewashed building with the brightly coloured yellow windows.

'It looks lovely, Hannah, doesn't it?' Her sister looked a bit doubtful.

Paddy was standing up ready to get out quickly. Katie went up to the school door with them, where a teacher welcomed all the pupils into a large open hall and began to tell them some of the things they would be doing during the year.

Katie had to stay outside but through the long window she could still make Hannah out, her white-blond hair making her stand out from the rest of them. They were singing, the sweet clear voices swelling together. Hannah loved singing.

Katie walked around the place. Through every window she could see bright classrooms, with coloured posters, painting sets, games and books. It was just the sort of school that her little brother and sister would love. She could go home now, they would be fine.

That night there was nearly a fight, with the three of them trying to tell their news and about their new friends all at the same time. Katie was proud of them, but in a way felt a bit deflated. Besides going with Hannah, she hadn't done much all day. She had brought Davey for a walk up to the shops and back. To be honest, it wasn't much fun just hanging around.

Tom didn't know what to do with himself either. He took Duffy for a short walk, and then he was up and down the stairs and seemed very restless.

Katie knew how he felt.

Chapter 15
THE UNIFORM

'Hi!'

Katie swung around. A plumpish girl in a denim jacket was walking towards her, pushing a battered-looking navy pram.

'You're a traveller too, aren't you?' she asked breathlessly. Katie nodded.

'My name's Sally, Sally Ward. My Mam told me she met your Mam down at the welfare office. We live at the back of Ashfield, our road is the Grove.'

The two of them fell into step. Sally wheeled her little sister Bonnie. Katie wheeled Davey in the buggy. Davey loved being on the move and chatted to every bird or animal they met along the way. Duffy ran on ahead, sniffing every gateway or tree they passed.

'How long have you lived here?'

Sally thought for a second.

'About three years, I suppose. Yeah, because Martin and Bonnie have been born since then.'

Sally was a nice girl, two years older than Katie and she seemed to have a great sense of humour. They walked around for about an hour, killing time. The baby had woken up and was looking for a feed.

'I'd better get home and give her a bottle or she'll scream her head off.'

Katie hoped they'd bump into each other again.

As it turned out, most mornings they did meet and fell into step. One day it lashed rain as they crossed the open green.

'Hey, Katie, do you want to come up to my house? My mother's gone off for the morning with my Dad.' They ran until they came to a house with a small caravan parked on the grass outside the door. Inside it was nice like their own house, but full to bursting with furniture and heaps of clutter all over the place.

Katie moved a pile of clothes for washing to get a space to sit down.

'Throw them over here, Katie. I'll do them later and put them out on the line before the others get in.'

'Sally, did you go to school?'

The other girl threw her chestnut-coloured hair back over her shoulder. Her green eyes sparkled and she opened her mouth wide to laugh, a strange mocking laugh.

'School! Yeah, I went to school – reading, writing, years of primary, I was the brains of the family and then we settled here and I got a place in the convent. Oh there was great excitement. My Mam and Dad were right proud. They got me a uniform and then the big day came.

'I went into that beautiful red-brick building ...'

Katie leant forward, anxious to hear about it.

'Go on, what happened?'

'I'll tell you what happened. I stood in that big school with its stairs all over the place and its long corridors. I didn't know which way to turn. None of the girls knew me and I didn't know them, so not one of them said a word to me. Not a word!'

'They must have said something.' Katie couldn't believe it.

'No. Not one word for four whole days. They walked in gangs up and down and I ... well, I walked alone. They knew I was different from them and they made it clear I wouldn't fit in. They realised it straight away and after four days so did I ...'

'Oh Sally.' Katie didn't know what to say.

'Don't you believe me?' Sally was upset.

'Of course I do.'

'Come on upstairs! I want to show you something.' Holding Bonnie in her arms, she raced up ahead of Katie.

It was clear that four sisters shared the bedroom as there were two sets of bunk beds. Clothes hung from the pine bedposts and a battered-looking pine wardrobe stood in the corner.

Sally grabbed the handle and pulled it open. She rooted through the racks and took out a wire hanger. The convent uniform – school blouse, white with small buttons, bright red jumper and navy skirt – hung abandoned from it.

'My uniform!'

Katie touched it. Sally sat on the bottom bunk, the uniform swinging from the knob of the open wardrobe door.

'I keep that uniform and every now and then

take it out and look at it.'

Katie felt embarrassed. She barely knew this girl and yet she was willing to share such a secret with her.

'Why are you telling me all this?'

'Maybe you should know, understand why I'm just hanging around.'

'But so am I,' Katie admitted.

'Listen, that uniform is a reminder of what might have been. I go over and over it again and maybe if I hadn't been so scared, maybe if I'd laughed and joked, maybe if I'd just given it five days or six days, been a bit tougher, just brazened it out, it might have been okay. Surely in the whole of that school there was one girl, just one girl who might have been a friend. I'm not that bad a person, am I?'

She turned to Katie, her eyes sad and a frown creasing her forehead. Katie felt totally at a loss as to what to do or say.

'Don't be sad, Sally, something will turn up for you.'

'Yeah, I can see it all ahead. Dossing about the place, maybe training, get a job in a factory if I'm very lucky and then before you know it I'll be married ...'

'You can't map things out just like that,' argued Katie. 'No one knows what lies ahead of them.'

'Well,' joked Sally, 'some of us have a fair idea,' but she couldn't disguise the bitterness in her voice.

'Sally, why in heaven's name do you keep that uniform thing if it upsets you like that?'

'You don't understand. There are times you need to be upset, to be reminded. Anyway I know at least I was good enough to go to school and get a uniform. Who knows, maybe Bonnie will wear it in a few years' time, maybe she'll get to do things I never did?' Her baby sister lay half-asleep, gazing up at her.

Something fell downstairs with a crash.

'Oh gosh. I'd better get down to Davey, he's up to some tricks.' Katie was glad of the excuse to get out of the bedroom and back downstairs.

Sally cheered up. They enjoyed the rest of the morning together. The heavy rain clouds had blown away and the sun was making feeble attempts to come out. At lunchtime Katie ran back home as Mam would be looking for her.

It was strange, but that afternoon Katie found herself walking in a round-about way towards the large Community School. It was set on a slope and from outside she could see the heads of girls and boys in various classrooms. The bell went and she sat by a garden wall. A few minutes later gangs of teenagers began to stream out. They were chatting and laughing and walking in groups. Some were collected in cars and others made their way to the bus stop about a quarter of a mile away. The rest walked. She recognised a few of them from her estate, and one of the girls even waved shyly at her. She blushed. It wasn't that she was spying on them, she just wanted a chance to get a feel of the place.

She turned for home finally and began to jog. Her heart was pounding, her breath jerky. It was just the running, she said to herself, yet she knew she couldn't deny the excitement she felt inside. Secondary school! – she was going to talk to Mam about it.

She'd be like the rest of them, provided they had a place and that they'd take her. Maybe it was too good to be true. Don't get your hopes up, Mam was always telling her. But at that moment her hopes were flying high ... as high as a seagull in the open sky.

Chapter 16
A NEW START

'Well, Mrs Connors, are you happy with what you've seen?' asked Mrs Quinlan, the Principal.

Katie could tell that her mother was ill-at-ease. 'It's lovely, Mrs Quinlan,' she interrupted.

Mrs Quinlan was very different from the other teachers she'd met over the years. Her blond hair was cropped short and she wore huge red-framed glasses that made her look like a big round owl.

'Now, I know you'll be at a disadvantage starting late, Katie, but as they say, better late than never.'

Mam was sitting very quietly. The huge corridors and classrooms and science labs and sports hall had taken her breath away, and they had only been shown a small part of the Community School.

Katie herself felt a little bewildered and hoped she would be able to find her way around.

'Here's your booklist. There's a second-hand bookshop in town, you'll get most of them there. This is your daily timetable and an information sheet about classes and after-school activities. A lot goes on here after the bell rings, you know.'

Katie glanced at it. Judo, dance, tennis, drama, hockey, computers – the kind of things you dream about doing but would never get the chance.

'Now, I'll show you the way out.'

She led them down a long yellow-painted corridor with a polished tiled floor. The wall was covered with framed photographs of hockey teams, a group of students dressed up as Vikings, two boys in judo outfits and a smiling girl holding a shining silver trophy. Katie slowed down and trailed behind her mother and the teacher, trying to read the inscriptions and dates. An image of herself holding a tennis racquet and smiling into the camera made her giggle.

They reached the main door and said their goodbyes.

'I'll see you here on Monday, Katie,' said the Principal, 'and remember to be on time.'

They walked back down past a row of parked cars. Katie could tell Mam was worried.

'Do you think you'll manage it, pet?'

'The rest of them do, so why shouldn't I?'

'But, Katie, we're not the rest of them. Are you sure you're not taking on too much?'

'Mam, stop worrying, I'll be fine.'

'Well, do your best and your Da and I will be right proud of you, one way or the other. Did I ever think I'd see the day when one of my own went to the secondary!'

*   *   *

On her first morning, Katie walked up and down the girls' locker room trying to find her locker. There were so many of them and every one of them grey! The key said number 102. Down at the bottom of the room there was a large mirror and a row of basins, and through a door beside these were the toilets. Crowds of girls hung around chatting and pushing and shoving, so that it was impossible to see which grey door was hers. A sharp bell rang and the crowd heaved towards the door and set off in the direction of the sports hall.

Number 99, 100, 101, 102 – great! The key was tiny and hard to turn, but she managed it. She stared in. The locker was so small! How would she fit everything into it? She hung her jacket from the metal hook and dumped the bag on the shelf. She tried to open the stiff buckle on the bag to find her timetable to see what classes she had. On her way in she had noticed timetables sellotaped on the insides of locker doors. She'd do hers tomorrow. She grabbed some of the books she needed and tried to push the locker shut. That stupid bag was jamming it. On Saturday in the shop it had looked ideal – now she wasn't so sure. One more push and she was able to turn the key. She followed the others towards the sports hall. The hall was packed and she manoeuvred her way to the back of the line where a crowd of her own age stood.

Mrs Quinlan was announcing something about an art club and a sponsored swim. Katie relaxed – it didn't concern her. She tried to pull the elastic on her ponytail tighter.

A boy with a book of names came down the line. He put a tick opposite each name.

'What are you doing here?'

'My name is Katie – Katie Connors. I'm new. This is my first day.'

He scanned the list.

'Well, you're not down here.' He stopped and stared at her. 'What year are you in?' He had raised his voice and a few heads turned to stare at her.

'First year.'

'Wrong line, this is third year. Anyway, you're too late now – get the first teacher to mark you in.' He turned and walked away, leaving her standing between the lines, in no-man's land. Then, as if by magic, the whole assembly turned around and started to make their way out the door. It was like a stampede and she was swept along in it.

Luckily, a few minutes later, Mrs Quinlan spotted her.

'Ah Katie, good morning. Now let me look at your time sheet. Yes, your first class is maths, that's upstairs in room 4. Mr Byrne will be taking you.'

When she reached the classroom door, Katie was tempted to take to her heels and run, but instead she took a deep breath and opened the door. Mr Byrne stopped in mid-sentence.

'Ah, the new girl. What's the name again?'

'Katie. Katie Connors.'

'Ah yes, I have it here on the list. Now find a seat for yourself.

All eyes turned and look at the new girl. A girl in the third row grudgingly moved a pile of books from the empty chair beside her and Katie sat down. Her name was Natalie, written in big letters on the book cover, and Katie noticed that she bit her nails. Her face was hidden by a curtain of straight brown hair which she used to avoid looking at Katie.

The blackboard was covered in numbers and Katie got out her pen and began to copy them down as the teacher explained what he wanted them to do for homework. As soon as the bell rang, everyone pushed back their chairs and headed out through the open door and down the corridor. Katie followed behind as they all went into another classroom. A tall, dark-haired teacher had already started class when she walked shyly in and was reading a passage from a book called *The Diary of Anne Frank*.

Natalie sat beside another girl now and avoided even looking at Katie. She whispered to her friend and they giggled. There were only two vacant desks, one on its own, practically under the teacher's nose, the other right at the back. Katie opted for the latter and sat down beside a boy with glasses and a rash of pimples all over his neck. He smiled at her, then turned his attention back to the teacher.

Katie listened too. She became wrapped up in the world of this girl Anne, hidden in an attic room.

The teacher suddenly stopped. He began to go around the class asking questions at random. Everyone seemed to know the answers and be familiar with the book. Katie hoped above hope that he wouldn't come to the back row, but like a strange homing device he must have read her mind and pointed at her.

'The new girl. Yes, I mean you – Katie, is it? My name is Sean Ryan. Now with our introductions over, will you be so kind as to tell me why Anne and her family were hiding?'

Katie could feel her mouth go dry. She had missed the start of the story and she wasn't sure. She tried to flip her memory back over his words in search of a clue. Two or three people tittered. The boy beside her coughed. Seconds were ticking away. The boy coughed again making her look slightly over at him and on his open pad he had written the word: *Jewish*.

Like a lifeline Katie grabbed the word. 'Jewish, Mr Ryan, her family, they were Jewish.'

The teacher, satisfied, moved on to question someone else.

A wash of relief flooded over her and she murmured 'Thanks' to the boy.

'My name is Paul. Welcome,' he wrote in large round letters in the pad. At the end of class he pointed her in the direction of the computer room.

It was miles away and up two flights of stairs. The girls – there were mostly girls – sat in lines hitting the keyboards. They were all so busy concentrating they barely noticed her slip into her place.

Katie sat down in front of a machine. Jeepers, she thought, I haven't a clue what to do. She had never used a computer before. The minute you barely tipped a letter with your finger it was printed up on the screen.

The teacher came up quickly.

'Welcome, love! Have you ever used one of these wordprocessors before?'

Katie shook her head.

'Well, I'll just set you up.' The teacher pressed two or three keys. 'Now, see those lines there?' She pointed to the screen. 'It is taking you through the start-up programme. Try not to use just two fingers. Here, spread out your hands, each finger on a letter. Try and type this paragraph, okay?'

Katie had to concentrate really hard to find the right letters. The others around her were quick as lightning. She'd never be that quick.

The teacher, a tall freckle-faced woman with an easy smile, came back every now and then to check how she was getting on.

It was lunchtime before Katie knew it and she had to rush down to the locker-room. She had a sandwich and a can of orange, but no one stopped to tell her where to go to eat. She spotted Natalie and a crowd of other girls from her class heading for a large room, so she just followed. The walls were covered in noticeboards with posters advertising all kinds of activities in the school. As she ate her sandwich, squashed on the end of a bench with a crowd of second- and third-years who ignored her, she pretended to study the posters.

The afternoon passed, more classes and more people and more rooms until the final bell went. One or two from her class nodded at her as they headed for the bus stop.

Mam was waiting to pounce on her the minute she got home.

'Well, pet! How did it go? Was it all right?'

Katie felt whacked. All she wanted to do was sit down and relax, but she could tell by Mam's face that she expected a blow-by-blow account of it all. Katie couldn't disappoint her.

'What about your class? Did you make any friends?'

'Yeah, Mam, I had lunch with a big crowd of them,' she lied, 'and we did computers and all sorts of things.'

Mam smiled. 'I've been thinking about you all day long, worrying about you. When we were young they used call us the Black Wagons and no one in the class wanted to sit near us. The teachers never paid much heed to us. I suppose they thought a few days in from the cold and wet was as much as we deserved. I didn't bother with schooling so I'm proud of you trying to get an education, Katie love. I know if your Da was here he would be too. He's just a bit ignorant as my grandmother used to say, but he has a family to make him proud.' Mam chattered on and on excitedly. 'I'm glad they were all nice to you in that big school.'

*   *   *

The next few days things didn't get any easier. She got some of her books second-hand and the headmistress gave her the rest.

The school day was so long. Most of the time she

just felt really tired.

'Knacker.'

'Tinker.'

She heard them, the names they called as she walked by. Did they think she was deaf?

Natalie and her friends began to hold their noses and say 'Phew, what a pong!' when they were near her.

The classes and the teachers were all right though. Even in a week or two she had learned so much. Her head was bursting with it all and she wished there was someone at home to share all this with. She was surprised to find herself saying, 'Francis would be interested in that', and 'I'll tell Francis about that in the summer'.

The boys in class never said much to her. Paul, who was about the nicest of them, would explain what homework she had if she didn't understand.

She especially loved PE. It was great to get a chance to run around and move instead of just sitting at a desk all the time. Also she could run fast and had good ball control. But when they picked teams for basketball, why was she always picked last? One by one the team captains chose until only the ones who were no good at sports and Katie were left at the bottom of the pile.

Funny, but once she started to play she didn't care how or why they had picked her. She just loved playing the game and could run rings around most of them. She tossed her long red hair in their eyes to annoy them.

'Keep your filthy hair away or you'll give us all nits,' Natalie shouted at her during one game.

'Cut it out, Natalie.' A strange-looking girl called Brona Dowling came over. She had short spiky hair and a row of earrings up one ear.

'Yeah, leave her alone,' one or two of the others added.

'Ah! Now we know why Brona's hair is cut so short,' jeered Natalie, flouncing off the court, pretending to scratch her head.

Katie was often tempted to just not go back to school, to shout, 'STUFF IT', 'I hate your school', 'I hate all of you', to walk out through those doors, but the thought of Sally and that uniform hanging like a ghost in her wardrobe haunted her. She would not be beaten. She was a Connors and her people had survived a lot worse than this crowd could imagine.

Chapter 17

GALLOPING

'A deserted wife, that's what she called me. She said I probably wouldn't have got the house if they knew those were the home circumstances.' Mam was almost hysterical. A new social worker had called as Miss O'Gorman was sick. The new person had got Mam all worried and she was convinced that someone was trying to get her out of the house.

'I told her Ned will be here soon, he wouldn't stay away that long. I'm no deserted wife!' Mam ranted on. 'These people are always trying to put people into boxes, I know what I am and it's not a deserted wife.'

Katie knew Mam was also worried about money as they had so little to manage on. There were gas bills and electricity bills, and rent to pay now too. Mam went door-to-door as often as she could around the estates and houses nearby. She always came back tired, but if she was lucky there would be some second-hand clothes and a few tins of food – usually beans and more beans and more beans. Katie kept hoping there might be a pair of black winter shoes in her size in one of the bags, but no such luck. Her old worn-out shoes would have to do.

Hannah let slip to Katie that Paddy was causing trouble on the bus. He wouldn't sit down and the driver was very cross with him. The teacher said one more incident and he'd be put off the bus.

'I don't want to go on my own, Katie, I know I have friends there but I don't want to go on my own.'

'Don't fret, I'll talk to him,' the older sister promised.

When she went into their room, Brian and Paddy were rolling around the floor mock-punching each other.

'Paddy, get up and stop messing!'

'Buzz off.'

'Get up. I'm just saying this once: no more messing on the bus or Da will give you a right belt when he sees you.'

'Yeah, well, he's not around.'

'He will be and I'll tell him. Mam's not well, she's upset at the moment and you're not helping one bit.'

Her younger brother just shrugged his shoulders and jeered at her. She looked at them, Brian and Paddy, how could two brothers be so different? When they were babies they were so identical that at first only Mam and Da could tell them apart.

Paddy had been born first and had always been the leader, the lively one, Brian was like a mirror image or shadow that followed him everywhere. He would always let Paddy answer first or talk when other people were around and yet when they played together they always seemed to be equals. Now they seemed to be going in different directions and it was affecting them both.

Three days later it happened. Paddy opened the emergency door of the bus and two of the other kids fell out. Luckily neither of them was hurt. But if the bus had not been stopped at the time or if the traffic had been heavy, things would have been much worse. So Paddy was off the bus for a month. He would have to walk all the way to school.

Things were going from bad to worse and Katie went to talk to Tom about it all. Her older brother was busy combing his hair and lacing up high canvas boots. She watched as he pulled on a bright new bomber jacket.

He swung around. 'What are you gawping at?'

'Nothing ... Tom ... Look, I'm worried about Mam. She's not well and she's scared we'll lose the house.'

He kept combing his hair.

'I never asked to be in this house,' he muttered under his breath.

'You never are in this house,' she shouted back.

'Look, Katie, I'm in a hurry. My pals are waiting for me up at the arcade.'

'Don't you care about Mam and Paddy? You could at least talk to him. You're his brother!'

'I can't do anything. I'll be late. I'm going.' He brushed past her and began to run down the stairs shouting goodbye to Mam on his way out the door.

'You don't give a damn about anyone but yourself,' she shouted after him.

Katie stared at his bed. A pale blue shirt that she

had never seen before lay discarded in a heap on the bed with his old jumper. Then she thought of the new jacket he had on. How come he had a new jacket when the rest of them had got no new clothes since the fire, only the cast-offs Mam got? She tried to block out her worst fears and suspicions. It would be just too much if Tom was in trouble too.

*　　　*　　　*

Galloping, galloping. She could hear the thunder of hooves in her sleep. The dream came again. The blue horse – she was about to touch it when she woke up, and a feeling of loss overwhelmed her. She was really thirsty too and decided to go downstairs to get a drink of milk.

The light in the kitchen was already on and Mam was sitting waiting for the kettle to boil. She had grey shadows under her eyes.

'So you're awake too.' Mam patted the stool beside her.

'I had another dream,' Katie confided.

'I wish I could dream.'

'Do you never dream?'

'I do, but usually only bad ones.'

'Are you okay, Mam?' Katie blurted out.

'Yes, Katie love, don't you fret. It's enough for one of us to be worrying.'

'What are you worried about?'

'All sorts of things.'

'Do you miss Da?'

'You know the answer to that, pet – we all do. Look at poor Paddy – he's lost without him and getting into trouble. And I'm afraid that Davey and Hannah will forget him altogether. And as for Tom – that boy can't look me straight in the eye – I'm uneasy about him. Maybe he should have stayed with Ned – a boy his age needs his father.'

'Maybe Ned was right,' she continued, 'maybe we shouldn't have taken the house. We would have found some way to manage. My mother raised ten of us in a wagon. We moved from place to place and camped wherever we could. Life was very hard in those days. Things were short. Many's the time we went hungry or walked barefoot. Times were hard – and it wasn't just us. The whole country was poor and yet people shared things. They weren't paying back big loans for houses and cars and videos and gadgets. They didn't chase us from their doors.'

'I know, Mam,' Katie whispered.

'You don't really, Katie. How is it I feel so bad sitting here in my fine big house with a good roof over my head and walls and windows to keep the rain and cold out? I who grew up in a wagon? Yet sometimes I feel the walls of this place closing in on me and I feel the floor above is going to fall down on me. I could scream and scream and not a sinner would hear me.'

'It wouldn't fall down, Mam, and the neighbours would hear you.'

'I'm like an animal in a cage – being held in, running from room to room, doing tricks. I swear I can hear the blood going through my head and my heart pumping. There's no one to have a laugh with or a bit of a chat to.'

'I'm here, Mam. You have me.'

'I know, Katie love, I know that.'

The kettle began to boil and Mam made a big mug of tea for herself. She took long slow sips of the hot milky liquid. 'I just wish that I was half the woman my mother was ... If only we still had our caravan, I'd have managed.'

'You can't turn the clock back,' Katie whispered softly.

'I know. If only I could. That fire – it was that fire that destroyed everything ... it destroyed us. And my blue horse gone, burnt to bits – every bit of luck we had is gone ... gone up in smoke.'

'Mam, stop. Please stop. You're getting too upset. Come on, we'll go back upstairs and try to sleep.'

Katie switched off the kitchen light and followed her mother up the stairs.

'Things will get sorted out, Mam, honest, they will.' She wanted to make sure her mother went to bed and followed her into the larger room. Davey lay sprawled across half the double bed. Mam pulled back the pink nylon quilt and blanket to get in, and she tossed her old dressing-gown on the bottom of the bed.

'Go on, love, away to bed yourself or you'll fall asleep in school tomorrow.'

Katie barely heard what Mam was saying. She stared at her. Mam was pregnant.

In a few months' time there would be another little brother or sister. She should have guessed. How did she not know? Another mouth to feed. How would Mam cope?

She hugged her mother and pulled the bedroom door shut softly behind her. Back in her own room she climbed onto her bunk bed and stared at the ceiling. No matter what she did she just couldn't get to sleep. Hour dragged into hour until it was morning. Every bit of luck gone, she thought, as she finally drifted off into a light sleep.

Chapter 18
WOODEN HEART

Monday was the worst day of the week. Putting on the navy school sweater and the shoulder straps of her bag across her back was almost like putting on armour and getting ready for battle. She would take a few deep breaths and hold her spine straight to control her inner panic. She got on well with some of her classmates and they would chat to her, and they raised no objections to her sitting beside them. There was another group who avoided looking her in the eye or talking to her, but who did nothing bad to her.

But there were about five in the class who never let up taunting her. 'Knacker', 'tinker', they whispered and jeered at her. She hated each and every one of them. Often she felt sure they must be aware of her heart pounding and of the crazy throbs of her pulse if they approached her. But she decided she would not cry even if her heart felt like a wooden heart. She often thought of the words of the song now, and she understood them! Would her heart fall apart, crack and split in two? But once she kept her eyes steady and put a damper on her temper, things passed off.

Natalie jeered and taunted her as often as she could. She made sure that everyone in the school knew that Katie was a traveller and tried to shame her at every opportunity.

'What's the point of the likes of you coming here?' she demanded to know.

Katie did her best to ignore her. At lunchtime one Wednesday when Katie went to get her sandwich, her locker had been broken open. It was the third time in a week, and this time her drink had been spilt down over her books and soaked her turquoise jacket which was covered with stains and flung on the floor. It was the only jacket she had. Her sandwich had been stood on, so now she had no lunch either. But the worst thing was that her new history book and Irish book the Principal had given her were destroyed.

It was only when Natalie came out of the toilets that Katie spotted a piece of squashed sandwich stuck on her shoe.

'You busted my locker.' Katie walked right up to her. Natalie refused to answer.

'You busted the locker and opened my can and spilt it and ruined my lunch.'

'I didn't touch your locker or your mouldy old cheese sandwich.'

'You did.'

'I did not.'

'I've proof.'

'The proof of a lying little tinker, is it?'

'The cheese on your shoe.'

'Anyone and everyone knows that the likes of you bring dirt and mess wherever you go.'

'I've brought no mess, you don't know what you're talking about.'

'Ciara, get her a mop and she can clean up her filth.' As she threw this order to her friend, Natalie snatched the can from the locker shelf and began to shake the dregs around the room.

Katie tried to grab the can but the other girl was taller and heavier than her and knocked her against the locker door.

'Leave her alone, Natalie.' It was Brona Dowling.

'Mind your own business. You keep out of this,' warned Natalie, flushing because someone had dared to question her authority.

'Don't clean it, Katie, don't mind her,' said Brona.

With her foot, Katie let fly and kicked Natalie against the wall of lockers opposite her.

Natalie then grabbed at a hank of Katie's long hair, swinging out of it. Katie felt as if her whole scalp was being tugged off and tears of pain stung her eyes.

She lashed out with her free hand, while with the other she tried to release her hair, but Ciara tripped her and she fell down on the tiled floor with Natalie on top of her. She tried to knee her off but Natalie was much stronger. She was pinned down and Natalie was just reaching for the can again when their maths teacher's voice boomed out.

'What the hell is going on here?' He stormed over and pulled Natalie off.

'Get to your feet, both of you. Up to Mrs Quinlan's office immediately. The rest of you stop gaping and tidy up here and go and have your lunches.'

Katie blushed scarlet. The boys were coming out of their locker room and began to catcall them.

'Hey, girls, who won the wrestling match?'

'When do you fight again?'

Katie's head ached and her shoulder was stiff. She noticed that Natalie's nose had begun to bleed by the time they reached the office.

Mrs Quinlan was furious.

'I will not have it! Two girls fighting like ...'

Katie almost laughed. She had nearly said the word 'tinkers'.

'Who started it?'

'She did.'

'No! she did.'

'She accused me of stealing her lunch.'

'You busted my locker.'

Mrs Quinlan came out from behind her desk.

'Mr Byrne saw the two of you fighting. Both of you have disgraced yourselves. Neither of you knows how to behave as a lady should. Natalie, last week you were in this office over remarks made about a teacher, and Katie, you know you are in this school under special circumstances. That temper of yours will have to be kept under control. I have a large school to run.

'We get bullying and beatings amongst the boys and I have to come down firmly on them, so it's only fair that you girls get the same punishment.

You are both suspended for two days. I will inform your parents. You will gather your things and I suggest you both go home straight away. I will see you next week in this office.'

Katie rolled up her jacket into her schoolbag. Maybe she'd get a chance to soak out the stains before Mam saw it.

*   *   *

The kitchen was quiet when she got in from school – the others wouldn't be home for nearly two hours. She found a note on the table under the sugar bowl. It was written in her brother's large scrawly writing. She read it quickly then stuffed it into her pocket and ran upstairs.

She was surprised to find Mam in bed with Davey lying near her, dozing.

'Ah, Katie, you're home early. We're just having a little nap.'

'I'm suspended, Mam.'

Her mother looked puzzled. 'What does that mean?'

'It means I'm not let back to school for two days.'

'But what did you do?'

'A girl was bullying me and we got into a fight ...' she trailed off.

'I knew it, Katie, you and that temper! It'll always get you into trouble!'

'Honest, Mam, it wasn't my fault at all.'

'How often have I heard that? Well, tell me then how is it you always end up involved in some way or another. You and Paddy, now the two of you in trouble. What's happening to my family at all?'

Katie wondered what she should do with Tom's note. Would this break her Mam's heart altogether? She decided to tell her and get it over with.

'I found this note, Mam. It's from Tom.' She handed the note to her mother who stared at it blankly. 'You'll have to read it to me,' Mam said.

Katie read it out:

> Katie
> *Tell Mam I'm sorry but I can't stick it here*
> *any longer. I'm going to find Da.*
> *If I stayed any longer I'd only bring the*
> *Guards down on the whole family. The twins*
> *will be glad to have the room.*
> Love
> Tom

Mam didn't say a word. She took the letter and held it close.

Chapter 19

EMERGENCY

Mam left the house early next morning with Paddy. She was going to walk the four miles to school with him to talk to his teacher. Hannah got the bus on her own. It was lucky that Katie was at home to mind Davey.

As soon as the others were gone she went up and began to make the beds. There were three spare sheets so she re-made the twins' and Hannah's beds. It was breezy out, a good day to do a wash. She filled the buckets with hot sudsy water. The washing took her the whole morning.

It was almost midday by the time Mam got back. She gave Katie money to go to the shops for some bread and a bag of potatoes and two cans of beans. Katie noticed that Mam's purse was empty. This was all the money she had left until she collected the children's allowances. Mam really wasn't well. Her face was pasty white. Katie sent the others out to play when they got home so the house was quiet.

By teatime she wondered if she should get the doctor, but Mam would have none of it.

'I'll just rest, pet, I'll be fine.'

The others were also worried and Brian blamed Paddy for making Mam sick.

It must have been about eleven o'clock that night when Katie heard Mam calling her. The minute she walked into the room she knew things were bad.

She lifted Davey from the bed and carried him still asleep and put him in Tom's bed. He never stirred.

'Mam, what is it? You need the doctor!'

'No, Katie. I'll have to go to the hospital. You'll have to get an ambulance – and quickly.'

'But I can't leave you.'

Katie stood in the centre of the room and didn't know which way to turn. If only Da or Tom were here. She slipped into the boys' room. Paddy was shifting in his sleep. She shook him.

'Wake up quick, Paddy!'

'What is it?'

'Stop asking questions, just get up, and don't wake Brian. Davey's asleep here too.'

'What's going on?' His cheeks were flushed with sleep and his ginger hair stood on end.

'You must get to a phone and ring for an ambulance. Mam's real bad and I can't leave her.'

'What's wrong with her?'

'I think she's losing the baby. Just stop looking at me like that, and for once do what you're told.'

A look of total confusion and bewilderment filled his nine-year-old face. He pulled on his tracksuit bottoms and a jumper and shoved his bare feet into his runners.

'I'll need money for the phone,' he whispered. There were no phones nearby but there was a public call box at the entrance to Ashfield estate, and in daylight hours there was usually a long queue to use it.

'I'll get Mam's purse.' It was empty.

Katie searched everywhere and at last found two 20p coins in Hannah's new piggy bank. She took them out and shoved them into Paddy's hand.

'Hurry up,' she urged him.

A minute later she let him out the hall door. She wondered should she run in next door and get Mrs Dunne, but instead she went in again and pulled the sheet off the living-room window and put the light on. It would be hard enough for an ambulance to find the house in this maze. She also left the hall door slightly open, with the light on there too. Paddy seemed to take ages. She got Mam a glass of water and two pain-killing tablets from the kitchen.

Big tears slid down Mam's face. 'I'm losing the baby, Katie. I don't think there'll be any saving it now.'

Katie didn't know what to say. All she could do was hold Mam's hand and sit and wait. Da should be here, she thought again, and a stab of anger so sharp that it hurt jolted her.

Paddy finally arrived back and ran up the stairs, panting and out of breath.

'They – huh – they – huh – are coming about ten – huh – minutes they said.' He stood bent over, trying to get his breath back.

It was another fifteen minutes, though it seemed like an hour, before Katie heard the ambulance turn into the road, its blue light sending flashing patterns around the room. Paddy led the two uniformed men up the stairs to the bedroom.

Straight away they took control of the situation. One of them sat on the bed beside Mam and talked gently to her.

'Now, my dear, we're going to have to move you.' They had a kind of chair-shaped stretcher and they helped her into it.

Katie and Paddy went down the stairs ahead of them and stood anxiously at the bottom.

It was a cool star-spangled night and the air was still. The blue light of the ambulance had obviously woken a few neighbours. Mrs Dunne was standing in her doorway in an orange dressing-gown and fluffy slippers, wondering what was happening. Katie held Mam's hand as they wheeled her down the driveway.

'I'll be fine, Katie, don't worry.' But Mam looked so ill, Katie felt sure she was going to die.

They lifted her up the step and put her onto a flat bed in the ambulance.

'Katie! You go with your mother, I'll stay with the rest of them.' Mrs Dunne was standing beside her.

'But I have to mind the others. If Davey wakes he'll want a bottle and Hannah will be – '

'Listen, pet, you go with your mother. I'll manage, don't you worry.'

The younger ambulance man had jumped in and was about to pull up the step. 'Are you coming with us?'

She made a snap decision and in an instant was

sitting opposite her mother.

'Thanks, Mrs Dunne. Thank you very much!'

The door slammed shut and the ambulance turned and moved off. Mam's eyes were closed.

'Are you there, Katie?'

'Mam, I'm going with you. You'll be fine, just relax.' She was amazed she could even speak. At this moment she felt as if she belonged in another world and that this was something happening to another girl and another mother, not to them.

The ambulance man took out a pad and began to fill in a form.

'Maybe you can help me with the details,' he said to Katie. She gave Mam's full name; she wasn't sure about her age and birth date.

'There are six of us, but two are twins.'

She told him how tired Mam had been the last week or so, also about the fire, about losing everything and moving to Ashfield.

He scribbled down some notes. He turned to Mam. 'Mrs Connors, are you all right?' There was no reply. Mam seemed to have fallen asleep.

He leaned forward and held her wrist.

'Joe, get a move on,' he shouted and banged at the glass behind the driver's head.

Katie reached for Mam's hand. It was cold. The man put another blanket over her. They were going so fast that to Katie it felt like they weren't even touching the road. Then they slowed down and turned in somewhere.

'Nearly there,' the man coaxed Mam. 'You'll be

in hospital in a minute, Missus.'

Suddenly they stopped and the door was flung open. The two men were out of the ambulance in a flash, pushing Mam in through huge swing doors towards bright lights.

Katie stumbled down after them. Her stomach felt sick, she thought she was going to faint.

Mam was disappearing in the distance behind a row of curtains. A porter at the desk just pointed Katie in the direction of a waiting room. There were two rows of chairs, and a huge television with a blank screen in one corner. A smell of stale smoke choked the air and made her feel worse. A bin overflowed with empty drink cans and cigarette butts. The room was empty except for a greasy-haired man down the end who was engrossed in reading the day's newspapers. A clock ticked over their heads. An hour went by and there was still no word of her mother. She went to the desk two or three times and asked the nurse, but all she was told was: 'The doctor is with your mother, so try not to worry.'

Finally a nurse appeared and sat down beside her.

'Where is your father, dear?'

Katie felt her blood run slow. 'I don't know. None of us have seen him for about six weeks.'

'Have you any idea where he'd be? You're travellers, aren't you? Would he be with his family?'

Katie shrugged. 'We moved into the house and he didn't want to. My brother Tom left and went to join him, and except for my Da phoning the welfare office to say that Tom was with him, we've heard nothing.'

'You do have a social worker, then?'

'Miss O'Gorman.'

The nurse jotted it down.

'Listen, Katie, your mother will have to have an operation tonight. She has lost a lot of blood and is very weak, but she'll be fine.'

'She won't die, will she?' Katie felt such a coldness inside as she asked the question.

'No! No! We'll take good care of her. Listen, you're all done in yourself. Sit there and I'll bring you a cup of tea.'

Once the nurse left Katie began to cry. Mam would be okay. She wouldn't die. God was so good. She searched for a tissue and found one crumpled in the pocket of her jeans. She had put them on over her pyjamas and her jumper was on inside out. She pulled it over her head and put it back on the right way.

'Now, here you are, love, get that into you. You've had a right old fright tonight.'

There was a cup of milky tea and a plate of pale golden toast. The nurse watched her take it.

'I've ordered a taxi to take you home. It will be here in a few minutes,' she added kindly.

'But I've no money for a taxi,' Katie blurted out. 'I have nothing on me to pay for it.'

'Listen, love, we can hardly expect you to get home like that at this hour. It's our treat, so don't worry about it.' Katie looked down, the nurse was pointing at her feet. God! she still had her slippers on!

'Come back tomorrow at visiting time. Your Mam will be upstairs in Unit 5 then.'

The nurse took up the plate and cup and left quietly.

A taxi man arrived in to the waiting room soon after, calling, 'Taxi to Ashfield for Connors!' He stared when Katie came towards him, but opened the door of the big car as if she was a person who was used to taking taxis everywhere. She told him her full address and he chatted away to her as they drove home.

'Delivered a baby last year in this car. All kinds of emergencies – you get used to them.'

Katie's eyes were almost closed by the time they drew up outside number 167. The taxi man walked her to the door.

The sky was beginning to brighten. It would soon be morning. Through the window she could see Paddy asleep on the couch. Mrs Dunne was sitting with her mouth wide open, sleeping too. Katie tapped the glass. The heavy-lidded eyes blinked open and the woman yawned as she stood up. She stretched as she opened the door.

'Well, Katie! What's the news?'

'Mam has to have an operation, but she's not going to die.'

'Well, thanks be to God for that. Now, if I go back to my own bed for the rest of the night will you be all right? The rest of them are asleep. If you need me, knock on the door and I'll be in here in a jiffy.' Standing up to go, she wrapped her dressing-gown tightly around her.

'Mrs Dunne, thanks. I don't know what to say.'

'Don't say a word, dear. I'll be around after breakfast and we'll have a chat then. The only thing is, the young fella is fretting thinking that he caused your Mam to get ill. For heaven's sake tell him she's okay.'

Before she went to bed, Katie crept over to Paddy and whispered: 'Paddy, Mam's all right. She's alive, she'll get well again.'

He mumbled something in his sleep. Too exhausted to do anything more, Katie crawled up the stairs and slid into her bed.

Chapter 20
THE HOSPITAL

Katie walked down the long corridor looking for Unit 5. The floor below was filled with beds containing smiling, contented women. Beside them stood little plastic cots on wheels, with small babies asleep in them. Cards and ribbons and soft toys cluttered every bed.

This floor was quieter. There were no babies here. Two or three heavily pregnant women walked up and down, chatting to each other. Unit 5 was down at the far end. Mam was in Room C.

There were six beds in the room, three on either side. Mam's bed was by the window. She was staring out at the city spread out below them.

'Hi, Mam.'

The face that turned to her seemed so like Hannah's it shook her.

Mam looked thinner, her skin was white and her hair loose around her shoulders. She seemed older and yet younger at the same time. She wore a short-sleeved white hospital gown.

Something hung from a metal pole over her bed. It was a bag full of red stuff and it was going through a long thin tube into a part of Mam's hand.

'Hello, pet.'

Mam reached to hug her but couldn't move because of her arm.

'It's blood, pet.' Katie looked alarmed. 'Some

person gives a pint of their blood,' Mam went on, 'and then they freeze it to give to the likes of me, would you believe it, girl!'

Katie stared. 'How are you, Mam?'

Her mother wouldn't look straight at her.

'I'm fine, pet.' She made no mention of the baby but she kept blinking as her eyes welled up with tears.

The lady in the bed beside shoved a box of tissues at Katie to pass to her mother.

'Let her cry, love, she needs to.'

Katie felt uncomfortable, so she stood up and walked to the window. The bed opposite was empty. Three of the women had men sitting beside their beds. The lady with the tissues had an elderly woman and another woman visiting her and judging by the resemblance, Katie decided they were her mother and sister. Mam only had her.

'Here, Katie, give me a hand to sit up more.'

Katie helped her up a bit and fixed the pillows.

'Oh, and Mrs Fox next door sent you in this.' It was a bottle of lemonade.

'Well, I don't believe it,' Mam said, and they both laughed.

Katie opened it and poured out a glass for Mam. The rest of the time all Mam wanted to know was how everyone was. Did Hannah go to school? Brian had PE today – did he wear his tracksuit? What about Davey, is he missing me? Is Paddy behaving himself? Who's minding them while you're here?

'Mrs Dunne. She's been real good and cooked a shepherd's pie for us for tea and she gave me the money for the bus fare here.'

All too soon a nurse went around and tinkled a bell to say visiting time was over.

She hated leaving Mam in this place but in her heart Katie knew it was the only place for her.

'I'll come again tomorrow, Mam.'

Her mother hugged her as if she didn't want her to go either. Katie waved back as she joined the throng of visitors moving towards the stairs. She wished Mam wasn't so alone. The other women all seemed to have lots of visitors and lovely nightdresses and plenty of things on the little locker beside their beds. Mam's was empty except for the glass and the lemonade. It didn't seem fair.

She missed two buses on the way home but was relieved to find that Mrs Dunne had finished giving the others their tea and had set Hannah and Brian to do the washing up. 'Your tea is in the oven, Katie.'

'Thank you again, Mrs Dunne,' she murmured as she went to the door with her.

'Think nothing of it. Your Mam's a nice woman, keeps herself to herself, 'tis the least a neighbour could do. How was she?'

Katie told her about the blood and about losing the baby.

Mrs Dunne crossed herself. 'I lost two of my own, but you just have to get well and get back on your feet and thank God for the children you have, that's what I say.' Katie nodded. 'Now go back in and eat your dinner before it gets cold on you.'

Late that night when the others were getting ready for bed, Paddy came in to Katie.

'Is Mam really okay?'

'Yeah, she'll be fine,' she tried to reassure him.

'Do you think I was the cause of it?'

Katie shook her head. 'No, Paddy, I don't. She wasn't feeling well for the last week or more.'

'I don't mean to cause trouble, I just – well – I can't explain it. Sometimes sitting in a classroom or on that old school bus, I feel like I just want to get free of it all. I hate being shut in, people planning every hour of the day.'

Katie stared at him, he was really worried about it.

'Paddy, being free and being a traveller is in your blood, you can't change that. It's just that some travellers can fit in and settle better than others.'

'Maybe I'm a bit like my Da or Tom?'

'Yeah, maybe.'

'Come on, away to bed.'

*   *   *

The next day she visited the hospital again. Mam had a bit of colour in her cheeks and was sitting up. A different woman was in the bed near her.

'I brought you a clean nightie and a hairbrush and some soap and a towel. Mrs Dunne sends her best wishes and the two old ladies who live across the road sent you this.'

Mam unwrapped the package. It was a tin of sugared fruit drops.

'Miss O'Gorman was in with me at lunchtime. I'll be going home in about two days' time.'

'That's good news.' They just chit-chatted until the bell rang. Mam was tired and needed to sleep.

As she walked up to the bus stop Katie wondered how things would work out during the week or two ahead.

There wasn't a penny in the house for food and she couldn't ask Mrs Dunne for any more. Maybe she should go and beg like Mam had to do at times when there was nothing left. She had just turned the corner when she spotted a familiar green car parked near the house.

She began to walk faster, then to run. It was!

Her father opened the car door and started to come towards her.

'My little Katie!'

She hurled herself at him.

He wrapped his arms around her and held her tight.

''Tis all right, pet, I'm back.'

'Why are you sitting out in the car?'

'Well, Tom told me where the house was, but I was just about to ring the bell when I noticed a strange woman there, so I wasn't sure if I had the right number and I decided if I waited one of you was bound to show up.'

'Oh, Da! You don't know how much we've missed you!'

She began to lead him up to the front door.

'Katie, where's your Ma?'

'Come inside, Da, and I'll explain it.'

A flustered Mrs Dunne opened the door with Davey in her arms.

'Mrs Dunne, this is my father.'

Mrs Dunne was disapproving and the girl noticed the older woman examining her father with curiosity. It would be the talk of the neighbourhood.

'How did the visiting time go? How is she, pet?'

'She's coming along fine,' Katie replied and added a 'thank you'.

The neighbour seemed anxious to stay.

'I'm fine, Mrs Dunne. Now that Da is here things will work out. Thanks again. Thanks very much.'

Mrs Dunne went off to her own house.

'Who is she? What's she doing here?' Da asked. 'What the hell is going on?'

'Mam's in hospital. She was real sick and had to get an ambulance. I went with her.' Bit by bit Katie told Da all about the panic of the last few days and all that had happened since she had last seen him.

Davey had climbed up on his knee and was busy pulling at the buttons on his shirt. When she finished, Da stood up and walked to the window.

'I let you all down and especially your Mam. My stubbornness got in the way ...'

Katie looked at him. He was the most handsome man she knew. His hair had once been black and was now sprinkled with grey, his skin was tanned from being outdoors, and his eyes were soft with laughter creases around them. She could understand how at seventeen Mam had fallen in love with him and married him.

'Hey look, here's Hannah and the boys.' Her father ran out and pulled open the front door and the others almost stampeded in to hug and greet him.

'I knew you'd come back, Da. I knew you'd never just leave us,' declared Brian solemnly. Hannah's eyes filled with tears the minute she saw him. He lifted her up and tousled her hair. 'How's my own little girl?'

Davey was pulling at his legs trying to get attention and jealous of the others.

Katie went to the kitchen and made a pot of tea while the others showed Da the rest of the house.

He opened the cupboards in the kitchen. It was clear there was nothing much there. He took a ten-pound note from his pocket and told Paddy to take the rest of them to the shops and get some food for tea and some cereal and bread for the morning. When they were gone he supped his mug of tea slowly.

'I'm sorry, Katie.'

She didn't know what to say.

'What made you come back, Da?'

'Well I was thinking about it. It's mighty lonely on the road without your woman and your children. It's okay when you're a young fella – look at Tom, he thinks it'll be a grand life. But when he appeared out of the blue, I knew it would break your Mam's heart. Then do you know who I met? That old one Nan Maguire and her grandson, Francis. She's a strange one.

'She told me I should be with my family now and not traipsing the roads of Ireland. She told me if I kept on the way I was going, everything I love would be lost to me. Well, you can imagine how I felt.'

'She has the second sight, Da.'

'Oh I know she has the gift. You have to take warnings from the likes of her seriously.

'So you decided to come back.'

'I just missed each and every one of you.'

'Where's Tom? Why didn't he come with you?'

'Well, he's a young lad that needs a bit of space. Maybe living in a town isn't the thing for him. He's on a site with my uncle Christy. He'll have no mam or sisters to look after him or hand him up a dinner, so he'll make his own way if that's what he wants. My guess is he'll be back before too long. Oh and by the way, young Francis Maguire was asking for you and he told me to give you a message – he hasn't forgotten.' Her father looked puzzled but Katie smiled to herself.

After Da tidied himself he was very nervous about going to the hospital to see Mam – you'd think he was a young fella going on a first date. And at the best of times he hated doctors and hospitals.

Katie would have given anything to have seen

the look on Mam's face when he walked into the
ward. Having Da back was bound to make things
better all round.

Chapter 21
TURNED AWAY!

Mam was kept in hospital for an extra few days as she had a bit of a setback. Da visited her twice a day and in between tried to make a few contacts around the area to see about odd jobs and collecting scrap. Katie took over the cooking and running the house.

The day that Mam came home from hospital Katie watched her get out of the car. She seemed to stop on the pathway, unsure if she wanted to cross the front door. She was so pale, and seemed almost to tremble. It was Da who urged and coaxed her inside and settled her upstairs in bed.

'I should be getting back to school,' Katie said to Da.

'Nothing wrong with staying at home for a while and giving your Mam a hand,' her father tried to persuade her.

She felt torn in two. Maybe staying at home wouldn't be so bad, school wasn't that hot after all.

Her whole mind was in a whirl. She wanted things to change and yet she didn't. If the truth be told, she didn't know what she wanted, she was like a piece of cork floating on the river, going any way it was brought, bobbing up and down, a silly useless thing. She hated her face, she hated the pimples on her forehead, she hated her clothes, she hated her hair. There was nothing she could do about most of it, but there was one thing she could change – her hair.

One Saturday morning Katie went up the town and stood in the main street. The weekends were always busy, people with lots of money busily spending it. Da had given her a bit of money for herself.

Music blared out from some of the shops, all the sounds pushing at each other, competing for custom. Women struggled in and out of the supermarket, many tugging enough bags of groceries to break an arm. Young children were already whingeing and wanting to be home ...

Jonathan's was the first hair stylist's she spotted. She read the prices on the list in the window. Yeah, she definitely had enough money, so she pushed in the door.

A tape of soft music played in the background. Two women were sitting with their heads leaning backwards at washbasins getting their hair washed. A girl, her hair a mass of bleached white-blond waves, was cutting a middle-aged woman's hair.

A tanned man with a moustache and a crisp white shirt tucked into tight-fitting jeans came towards Katie.

'Yes, may I help you?'

'I want to get my hair cut,' she said.

'Well!' he stopped and stared at her, taking in every inch of her, from her runners right up to her sweatshirt.

'We are very exclusive, our prices are steep,

especially on a Saturday.'

'I have the money,' she patted the pocket of her jeans.

'Well, it's not just that, actually we have a problem with your type of hair. I'd advise leave well enough alone.' He seemed embarrassed and fumbled over his words.

'What do you mean?'

'Well, it might just frizz up on you. No, I wouldn't cut it.'

Katie stared at him. 'But I want to get it cut, it's too long and it needs –'

'I've given you my professional opinion. I'm sorry, but no.' He turned on his heel and went back to a chair where a girl of about nineteen was sitting with a towel around her neck. He lifted up the hairdrier and turned it on full blast and began to blow-dry her hair.

Standing there on her own, Katie had no option but to step out of the shop.

About ten doors down from there was another hairdresser's called Clip 'n' Cut. It was a lot bigger than the last one and seemed much busier. There were about eight basins and each one was occupied. In front of a row of mirrors, women stared at their reflections. There was hair in every stage of mess – wet, greased, hair with bits of paper stuck on it and hair poking out of a sort of bathing cap in a frenzy of madness. Katie couldn't believe it. She had never seen anything like it.

The woman in charge came over to her. She wore

a well-cut suit and giant dangly silver earrings and looked friendly enough.

'Yes, what is it?'

Katie flushed. 'I want to get my hair cut a bit.'

The woman seemed surprised.

'Humph!' She waved back towards the busy shop. 'As you can see, I'm full up.'

As she spoke two women came in, nodded at her and went and sat down in a small row of chairs. They began to flick through glossy magazines.

'Will I wait then?' enquired Katie, starting to take a step towards them.

'No!' The woman replied sharply 'Those customers have already made appointments. You might end up waiting hours. Why don't you try somewhere else or come another day.'

As she spoke she managed somehow or other to walk Katie to the open door.

Katie felt deflated. She blinked and looked up and down the street. There were bound to be a few more hairdressers in a town this size. She had to walk for about ten minutes before she discovered another one. It was up a narrow stairs, over a florist's. Inside, Michelle's was busy enough. The women were older and sat studying their newspapers and magazines under big, old-fashioned hairdriers. There was a circle of cotton wool wound around most of the heat-reddened faces. One or two looked up as she came in. Obviously it was Michelle herself who, all of a fluster, came over to her. She was like a big pink marshmallow – her skin was

pale and she was squashed into vivid pink leg-
gings and a pink-and-white polka-dot top. She
wobbled over to Katie.

'Yes, dearie?'

'I'd like to get my hair cut.' Maybe it would be a
case of third time lucky.

'Oh, I don't know!' The woman walked around
her.

Two or three of the customers lowered their
voices and were semi-listening.

'Come over here and sit down a second.' She
called Katie to a plastic seat near a silver cash
register, opened a kind of glass box, took out a
long-handled comb and using the long tip of it
lifted up one or two sections of the thick reddish
hair.

'I don't like messing around with coloured hair,'
she muttered.

'It's not coloured, I've always been a redhead.'
Katie lifted a hand to her head.

'No, I would prefer not to ...' Her face was
pulled into a prissy look which she directed towards the women.

'My hair is clean, honest! It was washed two
days ago,' Katie pleaded.

'No. I think it's best to leave it,' the owner added
firmly.

Stunned and conscious of the glances of the
middle-aged women, Katie went bright red and
stood up and left. She felt totally humiliated. It
wasn't fair. She hadn't got two heads. She wasn't

a criminal. Did they think she'd steal or break up their shops?

She stood outside, staring in at them.

'Tinkers, they're everywhere,' she heard the owner joke.

How could it be? She stumbled back down the stairs. The sunlight outside made her squint. She tried two more places. One just shouted that they didn't want the likes of her, and the last wouldn't even open the door to her.

She felt sick to her heart as she stood at the bus stop. Certainly she couldn't go home straight away. It began to rain. Tears slid down her face and rain soaked her hair. Wet and heavy, it hung around her as she hopped on the number 26 bus. Maybe Sally would be home. She skipped the stop for her own road and went on another, to Sally's house. She rang the bell. Inside, a gang of children played on the couch.

'Hiya, Katie, come on in. They're driving me crazy. Mam and Dad are gone down to Wexford for the day to a funeral. Why is it always wet when I've to mind them?'

Katie followed her friend into the untidy, cramped kitchen.

'Jeepers, Katie, you look awful. What's wrong?'

Katie hung her head. She was ashamed to tell her friend what had happened.

'I thought I was going to get my hair done,' she said sadly.

Sally seemed puzzled. 'Changed your mind?'

Katie shook her head. 'Had it changed for me, more like.' She began to pull at the wet ends of her hair. 'I hate it, I hate it,' she cried.

'Your hair? But you've lovely hair, look at my old mop.'

'No, it's not my hair, it's everything, just being different!' Like floodgates bursting open, the whole story tumbled out. Sally was almost as upset as Katie and every time one of the younger ones stuck their head in the door she screamed 'Out!' at them.

'Look, Katie, just say "Sod them".'

'Sod them,' Katie muttered.

'Go on, louder. SOD them!'

Within five minutes Sally had her laughing till the tears ran down her face. Then Sally got out her mother's big kitchen scissors.

'Would you like a snip, Madame?' she asked prancing around the floor. She took a mirror down from over the sink and made Katie hold it.

'Now keep her steady. Didn't I tell you that if I didn't become a film star my next choice of career would be a hairdresser? So you'll have the privilege of being my first customer.'

Katie didn't know whether she was serious or not, but within a few minutes had agreed to let Sally shampoo her hair and give it a trim.

She closed her eyes to stop the mountain of bubbles Sally had lathered up getting in her eyes and she kept them closed while the older girl dragged the comb through the thick jungle of hair.

She dared not open them as she felt the scissors move across the edge of her hair. Her head began to feel lighter. She was half-afraid to look for fear of what she might see.

'All finished,' announced Sally.

Katie partially opened her closed eyes. Long wet strips of hair littered the kitchen floor. She looked up. Her hair no longer fanned out like a cape. It hung neatly in an almost straight line to the level of the breast bone. She shook her head and felt the new lightness as her hair swung freely from side to side.

'Sally, it's great!'

'I'm not sure if it's really straight, but I'll see better when it's dry.'

Just being with the other girl and sipping mug after mug of tea and talking about funny things that had happened on the road seemed to pass the time. After a short while Katie's hair was dry. It fell softly around her face. She peered in the mirror. She looked older and maybe even wiser.

Sally was using the brush and pan to remove every trace of hair from the floor. Thirteen years of growth was flung into the kitchen bin.

Walking home from Sally's, Katie felt more confident. She smiled at one or two people she passed and they even smiled back at her.

Mam was downstairs in the kitchen, folding a pile of clothes.

'Well, what do you think?'

Mam didn't look up for a minute. Then she ran

her fingers softly over Katie's head.

'It suits you real well, pet. You're growing up to be a fine girl. I'm right proud of you.'

'I've still got the money,' Katie declared.

Her mother frowned.

'Nah, don't worry about it, Mam. Sally ended up cutting it for me. I'll explain later.' It was such a relief to see Mam back on her feet.

Wait till she got back to school. Natalie wouldn't be able to grab her so easily again.

Chapter 22

SAWDUST AND SHAVINGS

First class was home economics. Cookery! I might as well have stayed home, thought Katie. She had no white coat, but she tied her hair back.

There were nineteen other girls and four boys in the class. The large, tiled, home economics room was set up with six cookers and six sinks, large work tables and stacks of cookery equipment.

Everybody had a partner already, so she was on her own. But she knew she was a better cook than the lot of them put together. Mrs Kelly began to write recipes for basic brown bread and pancakes on the blackboard. The rest of the class were busy taking down the recipes.

'Miss Connors, I suggest you write down the recipe like the others as you'll need the ingredients next week. Today I will demonstrate,' Miss Kelly told her.

Katie took up her pad and jotted them down reluctantly. When the teacher was busy showing them step-by-step what to do, Katie found herself day-dreaming.

A boy from fifth year stuck his head in the door. 'Mrs Quinlan wants to see Kathleen Connors in her office.' Having delivered the message, he disappeared straight away.

Every head turned to look at Katie. What had she done now? Gathering up her books she got off the stool and headed straight for the Principal's office.

Mrs Quinlan was sitting at her desk reading a book and drinking a cup of coffee.

'Come in, come in and sit down, Katie.'

Katie was wary.

'I just wanted to find out why you stayed out an extra week over the suspension period.'

Katie just shrugged. Family problems were not any of this woman's business.

'I'm not poking my nose in, Katie, I do care and I am concerned about you ...' she trailed off.

'My Mam was sick and had to go to hospital. I had to mind the rest of them,' she stated.

The Principal put down her book. 'It's important not to miss school. Pupils who are absent for whatever reason tend to fall behind. They end up putting a lot of pressure on themselves and, let's face it, there are enough pressures on you without loading on more.'

'I'm sorry, but Mam needed me.'

Mrs Quinlan just nodded. 'Now you're back I hope you will settle back to the school routine. You know I'm here if you need me.' Katie sensed that the woman was sincere. She guided Katie to the door.

'Now back to class!'

Katie looked at the clock, there were about fifteen minutes of home economics left. She went the long way round to the classroom, ambling along, taking her time. It was unusual not to have everyone else bashing into her. She was about to pass an open door when she spotted a few of the boys from her class engrossed in work inside.

It was the woodwork room, and she could hear the whirr of a saw. She stood watching for a few minutes. The teacher was going from bench to bench, and a scatter of woodshavings littered the floor. They were all so absorbed, no one seemed to notice her.

Totally out of impulse she turned back the way she had come and soon found herself outside the Principal's door again.

'Come in!' Mrs Quinlan called. 'Did you forget something, Kathleen?'

'No, it's not that, Mrs Quinlan. I was wondering, can I change subjects?'

'When?'

'Today. Now!' she blurted out.

'But you have home economics now. I really don't think it would be possible for you to join the French class at this late stage. Some of the students have done two years of French in primary school before coming on here, you'd just be lost.'

'No, Mrs Quinlan, I'm not interested in French. I want to change to woodwork,' she pleaded.

The surprised woman took out a file from her drawer. 'Woodwork, well, it's not exactly what one expects of a girl. Don't you think that studying home economics and learning about nutrition and how to budget and plan meals and so on would be far more beneficial to you and your family?'

'We do some of that in science, Mrs Quinlan. It's

cooking! I like cooking but I get enough of it at home. No, I fancy the woodwork, it looks interesting. That is, if they'll have me.'

'Well!' Mrs Quinlan laughed softly to herself. 'I suppose there's no reason to stop you changing. I'll talk to both teachers at lunchbreak.'

Katie held her head high as she left the Principal's office. Her eyes were dancing in her head when she flounced into class and got back to her place. They were all mad with curiosity to see if she'd got into more trouble.

*　　*　　*

She said nothing, but a week later she headed for the woodwork room instead of the home economics class.

'Go and sit with your partners,' Mr McKeown instructed them as they filed into class.

Partners again! Katie couldn't believe it. She scanned the room. There were only two girls in the group and they were sitting together at the back of the class. One was Brona Dowling. She winked over at Katie.

There was only one boy sitting on his own. His name was Rory. She had heard the others jeer him sometimes and Natalie always said he was a bit simple. Katie went and sat opposite him at the large woodwork desk. There was a little locker full of tools beside her. Everyone else seemed to know what they were doing and a gentle hum of conversation filtered around the room as they started work.

Rory spread a long plank of wood across his side and began to plane it. He whistled as he worked. She hoped the teacher would remember her and come over.

While she waited she looked around the room. It was large and airy and long windows reached to the floor. There were two huge wooden cupboards at the very back, with wooden shapes stacked on top of them. Diagrams were sketched out on the blackboard. On one wall hung a poster. Katie went over to look at it. It showed different kinds of trees from all over Ireland. She recognised every one of them. They had camped in woods, forests and meadows, by the sides of roads, in the grounds of big old houses – looking at this poster was like seeing a lot of old friends. Under each tree was a cross-section showing its wood-grain.

'Interested in wood, are you?' Katie spun around. Mr McKeown had come up behind her. She nodded.

'Well, I'm always glad to get more pupils interested in craftwork.' The teacher looked closely at her.

'I always loved trees. I used to hide in them when I was little. My Da used to have to send my big brother Tom to search for me. No matter where we were I'd find a tree.'

'You moved from place to place then?' He smiled.

'Yes, sir. I'm a traveller. Life on the road was hard, but, well, it was grand.'

'Never boring, I'd say. Now, Katie, a simple shape to cut out is a good start. The rules of this room are that no one touches that saw,' he pointed to a large circular saw fixed in the middle of the room, 'that is totally off-limits. I'll show you how to use the small fret-saws – and watch carefully. I don't want people chopping off fingers, I have no intention of spending my time putting on bandages and plasters.'

Katie had already noticed the large white first-aid box with its red cross in the corner over the sink.

'First off, I want you to leave your books outside.' She ran out with the small pile of books.

When Katie went back in he was standing at a noisy machine helping two boys to sharpen some tools. Sparks flew around them. When he'd finished he came back to her. 'Now, little lady, let's get you started.'

He arrived over with a rectangular piece of wood 'Now I want you to square this off.' He passed her a piece of chalk and a large wooden T-square and left her to it. She couldn't decide what size square to make and had to keep rubbing out the chalk with spittle.

'Do it fairly big, it's much easier,' Rory advised her across the desk they shared. 'We did them and then when they were sanded and polished we put our initial on them. Painted it on. It's only an exercise. Next week or so you'll make a rabbit.'

'What are you making?'

'It's a tray, a wooden tray for my mother. Later on I'm going to make a toybox for my brother Richard and if I'm able, a kind of doll's house for my two sisters. That'll be all the Christmas presents taken care of.'

Katie stared at him. This boy was very different from the Rory who stumbled around the school and whom the teachers gave out to constantly for not doing his work. He must have read her mind because he blushed. 'Woodwork's my best subject.'

Katie settled herself and soon became engrossed. She drew a 'K' on the wood too which helped dictate the size. Mr McKeown showed her how to use the small fret-saw. It was pretty difficult and the lines were jagged when she'd finished.

'Now, sandpaper all the edges until they're smooth.'

She loved the smell in this room. The scent of woodshavings and glue blended with the sweet smell of different sorts of timber. She just couldn't believe it when the teacher told them to tidy up as the bell would go in ten minutes. Katie was given one of the brushes and swept one half of the room. All the sawdust and shavings were put in a big bin. Then each of them had to make sure that every tool listed inside the door of the workbench lockers had been put back. As she walked out of class and Mr McKeown locked the door after them she knew she could hardly wait until Thursday and their next lesson.

Chapter 23

BACK ON THE ROAD

November days – always so dull and damp. Like a fog, winter had seeped in. By mid-afternoon the soft, hazy sun would disappear. The few trees in Ashfield estate had lost their leaves and stood spindly and bare, forming scary shadows.

'Come on, Duffy, let's go for a walk,' Katie said one Saturday. The dog ran on ahead, snuffling amongst the wet, mouldy leaves.

Katie headed up towards Ashfield Grove. She'd call on Sally. They hadn't seen each other for ages. Duffy was good company and wandered along beside her.

As soon as she turned the corner she saw that the ramshackle caravan was gone from Sally's garden and the glass on the large bedroom window was cracked. The house looked empty, abandoned.

She rang the doorbell again and again. No one answered.

'You're wasting your time, love,' the old man from across the street shouted at her, 'they've gone!'

'All of them?' Katie couldn't believe it.

'Yeah, just upped and left. Didn't even bother to lock the house up properly and the vandals got at it. Those type of people have no sense of responsibility, don't care about their neighbours.'

Katie stared at him and then back at the house.

She felt guilty. She shouldn't have waited such a long time before visiting Sally. She had been so caught up with school and homework and the family and herself. Now Sally was gone, back on the road and hadn't even bothered to say goodbye.

'Sally's gone, Mam,' she announced as soon as she got home. 'The whole family left. They must be gone back on the road.'

Mam was busy buttering bread.

'I'm not surprised, love.'

'Did you know? Why didn't you tell me? I never even said goodbye.'

'It was just a feeling. Mary Ward told me often enough that they were thinking of going back on the road.'

'More power to them, that's what I say,' stated her father, coming in the back door and leaving his muddy wellington boots on the doorstep. 'Getting out of that house is probably the best thing Paddy Ward ever did.'

'It's winter, Ned, there's not much sense going back on the road in the middle of the cold and wet.'

Katie stared at her parents. Somehow there had been a subtle shift in the conversation and she wasn't sure anymore who Da was talking about.

*   *   *

The darkness would envelop the house and sometimes it seemed as if the four walls of the house and the roof were a prison cell built to keep them in. Da would pace up and down before disappearing off into the night for a hour or two. During the day he would drive off to the local dump or any place which would be a source of scrap – he seemed to find it impossible to stay in the house for any length of time.

The minute they all came home from school the television was switched on and it was not turned off until bedtime. Strange voices and strange people held court in the middle of their living-room night after night. Katie found it hard to manage all the homework she had to do as there was only one table in the house, the kitchen table. She cleared the clutter off it and tried to spread out her books. Brian would take another corner. Sometimes she was just about to start when the tea would be ready and everything would have to be packed away in the bag until the last cup and plate had been washed and Hannah and herself had tidied everything away.

Sometimes Hannah would sit quietly looking at her books. 'You're real clever, Katie, I wish I was like you.' She still had trouble reading and Katie would often find herself reading a story or explaining some history or geography to her little sister.

'You make it sound so easy, Katie, I wish you were a teacher.'

It was hard to tell her to buzz off and it took Katie ages to get her own homework done. She was on her own and if she didn't know something there was no point asking Mam or Da.

*   *   *

Brian was getting on well at school, so it came as a

bit of a shock when he arrived home one day with a black eye. Katie was really surprised as he had never been a fighter.

'I showed him how to stand up for himself,' Paddy annouced. Trust Paddy.

'There's always a first time,' stated Brian. 'I'm not ashamed of what I am and I won't be insulted. I don't hide things. Next week teacher said he's going to do a lesson on travelling. One of the boys in the class used to live out in Saudi Arabia and he is going to tell them about that and I'll tell them about life on the road and living in a trailer. The teacher was pleased, but one of the other fellas beat me up.' Katie looked at her younger brother and wished for his courage.

Natalie still teased her. She wished she could laugh or pretend she didn't care or that it didn't matter to her, but it did. She tried not to let the others see her when she felt like crying. Brona always seemed to be around when she needed someone to talk to. She lived near Natalie, but paid no heed to her bullying.

'I know too much about that one for her to try it on me. Believe me, Katie, she has nothing much to be so full of herself about. Her family are a shower of wasters. Bullies like her always try to pick on people who are a bit different – they haven't the guts to do anything unusual themselves. She tried it on me when I got my hair spiked, but I put an end to it fast.' To Katie it seemed there might never be an end to it!

Chapter 24

TRIAL AND ERROR

'A rabbit would be nice.' Mr McKeown tried to persuade her, holding out the template of a round, fat bunny.

'I'd like to try a horse, sir!'

'Katie, what about a duck, or a train engine?'

He picked up each template and showed it to her.

'Don't you have a horse?'

He shook his head.

'I could draw one onto the wood myself.'

'Well, if you want to try it, but it's a difficult shape. Most people usually like the rabbit.'

She was about to say: I'm not most people, when he laughed and said, 'Just don't say it.'

She got two or three sheets of white paper from the back of the class.

'How's it going?' Brona asked her. Every Monday when Brona arrived back at school people had to be prepared for the unexpected. At the moment she had all her hair in tiny tight little plaits with multicoloured ribbons on each of them. Katie smiled and stopped at her workbench.

'Fine, thanks.'

'Do you like the hair?'

Katie couldn't help herself smiling.

'Yeah, nothing in the rules against plaits!' and she began to laugh.

Katie looked down at what Brona was working on. She was cutting out very small pieces of wood into triangles and circles and rectangles.

'Your jewellery?'

Brona held up a leather thong and a triangular piece of wood with a Celtic design in black etched into it.

'Great, aren't they! My brother will sell them on his stall in the market on Saturdays. This kind of stuff will go a bomb, won't it? Susan's making a few too.' Katie smiled at the bespectacled girl sitting quietly on the opposite side of the desk.

'What are you at?'

'I want to draw out and then make a horse.'

'Yeah, that would be right. You people are mad about horses aren't you?'

Katie tried to explain. 'This isn't an ordinary horse, but ...' She trailed off.

Drawing the horse was another matter. She had thought it would be easy. All her years had been spent with horses in some way or another. Now for the life of her she could hardly get the shape of one to come out properly at all. Drawing and painting had never been a priority growing up in the overcrowded trailer.

At last! She drew one that managed to look different from a big dog or a donkey. She was pleased with herself and longed to cut it out.

*   *   *

'Wrong, it looks all wrong.'

Disappointment swept over her. It wasn't right at all, it was too ordinary, too rigid. It was a horse so unlike the one she imagined and longed to create. Crestfallen, she stared at it.

'Katie!' It was Mr McKeown. 'Is there a problem?'

She looked at the simple silly horse shape. This was a stiff, heavy horse that would plod around a field pulling a cart, not the horse of her dreams, the one that came night after night unbeckoned, a horse that had travelled the length and breadth of the country and witnessed hail and rain and storm and heatwaves and snow. Silent through generations, it had watched over her family. This was a simple wooden shape, nothing more, nothing less.

'Well done!' He picked it up and turned it over.

She studied it.

'It's not right. It's not what I imagined at all,' she shrugged.

He stared at her.

'This is very good work, Katie, don't take that away from yourself! What is it for?'

He wouldn't understand. 'It was meant to be for my Mam, for our family.'

'Well, I'm sure they'll love it.' He passed it back to her.

'I think I'll give it to my little brother Davey, he likes horses. He can play with it.'

'That's nice.' He was about to turn away from her. 'But I want to make another horse, sir, this time more rounded, more shaped, a proper horse not like a cardboard cut-out one. Better than this.'

'Almost carved,' he murmured.

'That's right! Can I try again?'

'It's a lot of work.'

'I want to make it, sir, it's real important.'

'What kind of horse are we talking about, Katie?' He stared at her quizzically.

'A blue horse, sir.'

'Is there such a creature?'

'There was,' she said, then corrected herself, 'there is, sir.'

'Not a real horse then, Katie, but an imaginary one.'

'It's the horse of my dreams.' She hoped he wouldn't laugh at her.

'Well ... every girl is entitled to her dream. How about we make a start next week?'

It was a funny thing, but finally she could sleep at night. The walls no longer came in on her, the blue horse, if it did appear, was no longer crazed. It still enjoyed a run in the wind, but it also liked to stand in the shade and gaze at the vast meadow and chew the grass. It would swish its tail at the flies. It just enjoyed being.

*   *   *

Christmas came and went. They put a small pine tree in the corner of the living room. Hannah and Paddy made all kinds of decorations at school and hung them from it. There was a new doll for Hannah, a small blond mirror-image of herself, which had been christened Alice. Davey loved the simple wooden horse Katie had made. Paddy and Brian got a set of racing cars and a game. Katie got a book token from Mam and Da. They would never be able to pick out a book for her – this way she had hours of choice ahead.

Being under a good dry roof while the wind and rain howled around outside was a great feeling. And when snow fell in January, the small council house seemed suddenly huge and warm and safe.

Katie smiled to herself. Even a few months ago she would never have thought of this place as home. Now it was a safe haven at the end of the day. The memory of last summer, and the campsite and Francis and his goats seemed almost a century away.

Brona had invited her to a party in two weeks' time. She was so excited, but also worried about it. None of the rest of them in school knew it was her first time ever being invited to a party. She fretted about what she was going to wear and what Brona would like as a present – you had to bring a gift and she wanted it to be right – but despite these fears nothing would stop her going.

* * *

'Stop!'

She got such a fright she nearly dropped it.

'Don't do one more thing with it or you'll ruin it.' Mr McKeown was striding over to her.

'One thing you've got to learn, girl, is never overwork something. Take it a step too far and often you just destroy it.'

Reluctantly Katie put down the chisel. Maybe one of the legs was still a bit too wide? Maybe she should narrow it more? The tail a fraction too long?

The teacher seemed to read her mind.

'It's perfect, not one thing more.'

'But ...' she began.

'Katie, trust me. You've had four attempts. This is the perfect one!' he insisted.

'It's beautiful, Katie.' Rory stopped his work and gazed at it too.

The horse stood on the worktable in front of her. It was perfect. She knew every inch of it. Time after time she had closed her eyes and run her fingers over it till it felt right.

'Tomorrow I'll paint it,' she decided.

'Do you have to, Katie? The wood is so lovely. You'll ruin it putting a coat of paint on it.' The teacher tried hard to persuade her to change her mind.

But she was adamant – blue.

Often she wondered how her great-grandfather had originally begun to paint a blue horse on the wagons and carts he made. Perhaps he had dreamt of one too. A horse that came in the night and yet was the colour of the morning sky.

The others in the class gathered around. It was usual to view and comment on each other's work. She felt embarrassed and longed to be out of the room, and yet a part of her was proud of this piece of wood. Her first real carving.

'Phew, it's just –' Katie could feel her mouth go

dry – 'it's brilliant.'

'Well done!'

'Not bad.'

'You're so talented, Katie,' Brona winked at her. 'It's better than any tinker horses I've ever seen.'

'You're so lucky to be so good.'

She stood there, her heart beating. She rubbed her hands quietly together. The skin on her fingers was rough.

'Thank you,' was about all she could manage to say to a classful of smiling faces.

Chapter 25
THE BLUE HORSE

'Go on, Mam, open it!'

She could hardly bear this moment now it had come.

Everyone had been sitting quietly watching television when Katie ran upstairs, pulled the big white plastic bag out from under the bed and carried it downstairs. She laid it in front of Mam.

'What is it, girl?' Mam wondered.

'Open it!' shrieked the twins.

'Let your father do it,' Mam offered.

'Kathleen, get on with it,' Da urged.

The bag was coming off. She could see the tip of his ears, his nose.

'What is it?' pleaded Hannah, pushing between the others to see.

'A horse! Oh my God! It's my blue horse.' Mam could hardly speak. Her eyes met Katie's.

'Thank you. How can I thank you? It's so beautiful, just like the old one. Perhaps,' she felt it, 'even better! Did you make it all yourself?'

Katie began to tell how she drew it first and then tried to cut it out, but she could tell that nobody was listening. Mam held the horse close to her, studying it. Then they all took a turn to pet it and stroke it before Mam let Da place it on the windowsill where the moonlight shone in on it.

'Rest easy there for the moment,' Da told it –

you'd nearly think it was a child he was talking to.

'It'll bring us luck, Katie. I can almost feel it already.' Mam was smiling. 'No matter where we stop or where we travel, it doesn't matter where we roam, it'll stay with us. A sign for all the world to see that the Connors family will go on and on. Nothing will get the better of us.'

The blue horse stood still staring out through the glass. Beyond these walls were fields and roads and mountains and forests and winding cliff paths and clear cool streams.

Katie looked at it. The blue horse was home.

Other books by
MARITA CONLON-McKENNA

CHILDREN OF THE FAMINE TRILOGY

UNDER THE HAWTHORN TREE
Ireland in the 1840s is devastated by famine. When tragedy strikes their family, Eily, Michael and Peggy are left to fend for themselves. Starving and in danger of ending up in the dreaded workhouse, they run away. Their one hope is to find the great-aunts they have heard about in their mother's stories. With tremendous courage they set out on a journey that will test every reserve of strength, love and loyalty they possess.

Paperback €6.95/STG£4.99/$5.95

WILDFLOWER GIRL
At the age of seven, Peggy made a terrifying journey through famine-stricken Ireland. Now thirteen, and determined to make a new life for herself, she sets off alone across the Atlantic to America. Will she ever see her family again?
An extraordinary story of courage, independence and adventure.

Paperback €6.95/STG£4.99/$5.95

FIELDS OF HOME

For Eily, Michael and Peggy the memory of the famine is still strong. But Mary-Brigid, Eily's first child, has the future to look forward to. What kind of future is it? Ireland is in turmoil, with evictions, burnings, secret meetings and land wars. Eily and her family may be thrown off their farm, Michael may lose his job in the big house, and Peggy, in America, feels trapped in her role as a maid. Will they ever have land and a home they can call their own? Eily, Michael and Peggy have once shown great courage – now their courage is needed again.

Send for our full-colour catalogue